Shirreffs
The cold seas beyond
313

THE COLD SEAS BEYOND

THE
COLD SEAS
BEYOND

by

Gordon D. Shirreffs

THE WESTMINSTER PRESS
Philadelphia

LIBRARY OF CONGRESS CATALOG CARD No. 63–10333

PUBLISHED BY THE WESTMINSTER PRESS ®

PHILADELPHIA 7, PENNSYLVANIA

PRINTED IN THE UNITED STATES OF AMERICA

1

BOB DUNBAR opened his eyes and stared up at the dimness of the deck above his bunk. The waters of Dutch Harbor lapped steadily against the sides of the *Otter*. Now and then the ninety-eight-foot craft creaked a little as she swung at her anchor. Beyond that it was quiet. Bob glanced at his watch. It was a few minutes past five A.M. He closed his eyes and tried to drop off to sleep, but it was no use. It was just too quiet. There was a brooding uneasiness in the air.

Bob thrust his legs out from beneath the warm blankets, shivering as his bare feet hit the cold deck. He dressed quickly, glancing at his buddy's bunk. Gary Lunt was sound asleep. Nothing, but *nothing*, ever bothered Gary Lunt. Nels Andreason, another of the crewmen aboard the *Otter*, was muffled in his blankets, without even his thatch of blond hair showing. Farther aft was where Baldy Barker, the cook, bunked, and his snoring was as gentle as the murmuring of a trout stream.

Bob climbed up the ladder to the raised deck aft of the pilothouse and shivered again as the cold predawn breeze swept across the dark harbor. Something moved beside the starboard powered lifeboat and Bob inadvertently jumped. Then he recognized the solid, squared-off bulk of his uncle Mack Dunbar, owner and skipper of the *Otter*.

"What's up, kid?" asked Mack Dunbar.

"Me," said Bob dryly. "I couldn't sleep."

"Go back to your bunk."

Bob eyed his uncle. "What are you doing up?" he asked.

Mack tamped his pipe with his thumb. "Nothing at all, kid. I just wanted a smoke."

"At five o'clock in the morning?"

"Two bells!" corrected Mack. He snapped a match on his thumbnail and held the flame to the pipe bowl, sucking in on the pipe. The rich odor of the tobacco smoke drifted to Bob. Mack Dunbar eyed Bob through the light of the match and the smoke. "Go forward and check the anchor cable," he said.

Bob nodded. He slid down the ladder to the well deck forward of the superstructure and walked to the slightly raised deck at the bows of the *Otter*. He looked back through the dimness to see his uncle watching him, the alternate glowing and dying away of the burning tobacco now lighting, now hiding, his bronzed face. There was something wrong — something that Uncle Mack had sensed, as Bob had sensed. Dutch Harbor was a long way from the fighting war in the Pacific, a war that had been going on for six months after the "stab in the back" at Pearl Harbor. Dutch Harbor, on Unalaska Island at the easterly end of the long sickle of the Aleutian Islands, was a naval base, although there were hardly enough naval craft in the harbor to dignify it with that title.

He peered through the darkness toward the dim outlines of other craft in the harbor. He knew them all by sight—the seaplane tender U.S.S. *Gillis*, destroyer U.S.S. *Talbot*, the submarine S-27, and the Coast Guard cutter *Onondaga*. There were two Army transports in the harbor as well, the *President Fillmore* and the *Morlen*. There

6

were other miscellaneous small craft, besides the old, beached barracks ship *Northwestern*. A number of PBY's, naval amphibious planes called Cats — short for Catalinas — were also moored in the harbor.

The *Otter* was riding well at her anchor. She was always well-behaved. Bob had sailed as a hand on her every summer vacation from high school and knew every inch of her like the palms of his hands. Ninety-eight feet long, built of the best Douglas fir, with stem and frames of oak, sheathed with an outer layer of Australian ironbark, one of the hardest woods known to man, she was capable of being driven at twelve knots top speed by her single diesel engine and had a cruising range of three thousand miles. Her two thick, rather stumpy masts were ketch rigged to save on fuel, or to steady her at sea. *Otter* was not particularly handsome, as sleek-lined vessels go, but there was a feeling of power and usefulness in her high bulwarks, well-developed sheer, rather bluff bows and wide midsection.

Bob padded aft and climbed the ladder to the boat deck aft of the pilothouse. "All secure, Skipper," he said.

Mack Dunbar nodded absently as he looked to windward. There was the faintest suggestion of light in the eastern sky.

"I'll start some java," said Bob.

"No, kid. Wait. Stay here with me." There was a hidden urgency in Mack's voice.

"What's wrong?"

"I don't know. It's like the last war, Bob. A man develops a sort of sixth sense. Something awoke me this morning. I can't say what it was, *but it was there.*"

Bob nodded. It was the same feeling he had had. The sky was barely lightening. High, high overhead was a

7

cloud ceiling, thousands of feet in altitude. It promised to be a fine day.

Minutes ticked past. The wind shifted and *Otter* swung to head into it. Bob could plainly see a seaplane tender now. Something was doing on the *Gillis*. A light flashed. Men's excited voices carried clearly across the water, but Bob could not distinguish what they were saying.

" Go make that pot of joe, kid," said Mack Dunbar.

" Wait! " uttered Bob tensely. " Something's going on over at the *Gillis*! "

The wind shifted again and a moment later from somewhere onshore an air-raid alarm began its banshee wailing, echoing across the harbor, rebounding from the rugged heights about the harbor, seemingly awakening other alarms. Lights flashed on at Fort Mears and on the various ships in the harbor.

" Alert! " said Bob excitedly.

" Hold on," said his uncle. " May be a practice or a false alarm. We'd better get the crew up, though."

There was no need to alert the tiny crew of the *Otter*. Nels Andreason was first on deck, followed by Baldy Barker and Gary Lunt.

" Is it the real McCoy? " demanded Baldy.

" We don't know," said Mack quietly. " But there's nothing we can do about it. We can't run and we can't fight back."

It was then that Bob remembered, with an icy feeling in the pit of his stomach, that they were waiting for engine parts to be brought in from Kodiak and that without those parts the engine could not be operated.

" Steady," said Mack Dunbar. " If you like, you can take one of the boats and go ashore until the alert is over."

" What about you, Skipper? " asked Nels.

8

The skipper blew out a smoke ring. "*Otter* is my home, my business, my life. I stay with her." In the silence that followed his statement he looked at his crew. Not a man *or* boy moved.

Baldy Barker at last broke the silence. "I'd better get a pot of joe started," he said. He vanished below.

"Any orders, Skipper?" asked Nels.

Mack Dunbar smiled. "Lower the windows in the pilot-house so they won't shatter and spray glass all over. Gary, you check the pumps. We might need them. Bob, get out a spare line or two in case we go adrift. Might want to heave out another anchor."

Time flicked past. The sirens had stopped, but the activity went on. Gun crews on ship and on shore stripped canvas from their guns, elevated them, and traversed them to warm up the grease. The bigger ships in the harbor were getting up steam, preparatory to leaving for the open sea. It wouldn't do to be caught in the harbor, concentrated for an easy target. The crews of the ships were at General Quarters. As yet the All Clear had not sounded.

Once the activity of getting ready for the air raid — if there was to be an air raid — was over, there was nothing to do but stand around and wait. It was the old service game: hurry up and *wait*.

For some peculiar reason, Bob was more concerned about the *Otter* than he was about himself. As Mack Dunbar had said: "*Otter* is my home, my business, my life. I stay with her." Mack could have retired years ago, comfortable with his Navy pension, but he could no more stay away from the sea than a gull can. He had served in the Navy from the age of sixteen until he had put in his thirty years, seeing active duty on a subchaser in the Mediterranean during World War I, earning the Navy Cross, and later serving on various Antarctic and Alaskan expeditions. No one knew the Bering Sea and adjacent waters better than Mack Dunbar. He had stayed ashore for a few years, trying to adapt himself to the land, but it had been no use. He had bought *Otter* at a good price and had spent most of his savings to rebuild her to his specifications, and in her he had returned to the sea. Sometimes he went sealing, or fishing, did a little salvage work, or perhaps chartered her out for various hunting and scientific expeditions. This was Bob's third season aboard her, but this time he would not have to return to high school. He had been graduated with his partner, Gary Lunt, and although the two of them had wanted to enlist in the Navy, they were not quite old enough. The next best thing was to return aboard the *Otter*, where good hands were needed because of the man-power shortage of the war.

Gary Lunt came up on deck with a grin on his freckled face. " I was just thinking," he said with a chuckle, " that our mothers thought it would be all right for us to work aboard the *Otter* because it would be safe enough in these waters."

"Well, it looks as if it is," said Bob. He shook his head.

It was clearly light now, with the cloud layers about ten thousand feet above the island. Two hours had passed since the alert. None of the larger ships had cleared the harbor. Bob started for the ladder that led down to the well deck and missed the first two steps when a gun thudded off somewhere on land, to be followed instantly by the thudding of other guns on land and on the ships. Bob turned to look up at the sky, and as he did so something exploded between *Otter* and one of the transports, hurling a mass of blue water high into the air. Some of the water splashed on the clean decks of the *Otter*. Bob skidded on the wet deck and fell heavily. As he did so, he looked up at the sky again. Antiaircraft shell puffs dotted the clear sky high beyond the cloud layer in a ragged line. There was something else up there too, something upon which the morning sun glinted sharply. Enemy aircraft!

As Bob got to his feet and looked about for a place to run, a thought flashed through his mind. *There are no foxholes on the deck of a ship!*

Guns were flashing and roaring from ships and shore batteries. Even automatic weapons were firing, a battery of Army 37mm. guns was firing from the decks of the big *Fillmore*, though Bob knew the Japanese aircraft were three times beyond the range of those little guns. More bombs exploded in the harbor and on the land. The once-clear sky was filthy with shell smoke. Bob looked longingly at the shore. The water was icy cold, but he'd risk the swim if he had to.

Even with his fright, there was a feeling of wild exhilaration within him. Gary Lunt slid down the ladder and dropped flat on the wet deck. "Our mothers should see us now," he crowed.

Mack Dunbar stood on the upper deck, big hands clutching the railing, pipe clamped in the corner of his mouth, head tilted back, watching those motes of enemy aircraft high in the sky, almost hidden from sight behind the puffs of shell smoke.

Nels Andreason grinned at the two boys from the port wing of the little bridge. "We're safe enough if this is the best they can do," he said. "They must be from aircraft carriers."

"Haven't we got any planes based here?" asked Gary.

"Over at Cold Bay and Otter Point they have some P-40's," said Nels. "Maybe some bombers too, for all I know."

"They ought to be up there," said Gary.

"They probably are," remarked Nels.

A bomb erupted mud and water, hurtling it high above the stumpy masts of the *Otter*. Gary and Bob dived for cover as the stinking mud and dead fish splattered down on the *Otter*. Baldy Barker dashed out of the galley waving a meat cleaver. "Lemme at 'em!" he screamed hoarsely. "Come down and fight like men!" He stepped on a fish and ended up in the scuppers, still screaming fight and fury.

"Take it easy, Baldy!" called down Nels. "Gather up them fish! Them Japs is serving dinner for us, mate!"

"Look!" called out Mack Dunbar.

One of the silvery craft high in the smoky sky had dropped from the formation of bombers and was turning over and over, lazily, or so it seemed, drifting down toward the ocean.

"Scratch one Nip!" said Nels.

Then, almost as quickly as it happened, the raid was over, the tiny silvery motes in the sky had turned away and the shell smoke drifted off downwind. The gunfiring died away and the echoes did too, while the smoke from the guns rifted over the blue waters of the harbor, but there was other smoke rising from the land. The Japanese bombs had done some damage. None of the ships seemed hurt.

Half an hour passed before the All Clear sounded.

"Secure," said Mack Dunbar. He took his pipe from his mouth. "Get out the swabs and buckets! Wash down fore and aft! We were lucky, mates! Get moving there!"

Gary stood up and grinned at Bob. "Didn't take Barnacle Bill long to get his voice back into action."

"What was that?" roared Mack Dunbar.

"Nothing, sir! Nothing at all, sir! Just thinking out loud, sir!" said Gary, knuckling his forehead.

There was a grin on the face of the skipper as he went below.

A powered whaleboat foamed toward *Otter* as the boys finished swabbing down.

"Any casualties?" called out a young naval officer.

"None, sir," said Bob.

"Any damage?"

"Nothing a swab can't take care of, sir."

"You were lucky."

"What was the score?" asked Gary.

"We lost about twenty-five men," said the officer. "Soldiers and sailors. Shot down one of their bombers. We heard the P-40's from Otter Point got two of them, but it hasn't been verified."

"Do you think they'll be back?" called out Nels from the bridge.

"We hope not, but I wouldn't bank on it. There are Jap carriers within striking distance. We don't know how many of them there are, but the guess is that they have at least two of them out there in the fog somewhere, which is two more than we have. You'd better abandon that tub and go ashore. They might be back."

Nels grinned. "This ain't no tub, mister! And I thought that raid was fun!"

"No accounting for tastes."

The whaleboat passed out of shouting range and was gone.

Mack Dunbar came up on deck. "We can't leave Dutch,"

13

he said quietly. "If you boys want to go ashore, it's all right with me."

As before, not a man or a boy moved. Mack smiled and began to fill his pipe.

The long day finally passed. The chance that the repair parts for *Otter*'s engine might come in was a million to one. There was a chance too that shipping would be held back from Dutch Harbor as long as there was a threat of another air raid. There was nothing for *Otter* to do but swing uneasily at her anchor, and nothing for her crew to do but pace uneasily up and down her decks.

Mack Dunbar set an anchor watch that night. Every ship and shore installation was in readiness for another raid. The harbor was blacked out and through the short darkness of the summer night came the sound of moving trucks and the muted voices of men. The shore fires had been extinguished, but the cloying odor of the smoke still hung over the harbor, thinned by the night wind.

The crew of the *Otter* were up long before dawn. As soon as they had their coffee and breakfast, they extinguished the galley fire for fear of fire if the *Otter* was struck. They could see very little through the darkness, but they knew there had been little sleep that night and dawn in Dutch Harbor.

Mack paced the upper deck. Now and then he looked shoreward and once he came to the bridge and quietly said, "It's a wonder to me they didn't hit those oil tanks ashore."

"Maybe they're empty," said Gary.

"No," said the skipper. "The Navy tanker *Brazos* topped them off not too long ago. Over twenty-two thousand barrels of oil. If a bomb hits one of them . . ."

Even as he spoke an air-raid siren began to wail, as it

14

had done the dawn before. The weather was fair and the ceiling was high.

A cold finger seemed to trace its way slowly and deliberately down Bob's back. There was nothing to do; absolutely nothing to do but stand there on the deck of the little vessel and wait for whatever the enemy had in store for them. The last thing Bob did, before he pried his mind away from it, was to look shoreward toward those huge oil tanks, with his uncle's words etched on his memory. *If a bomb hits one of them . . .*

The attack came almost as though the enemy were maintaining a split-second schedule. Again the cloud ceiling was high over the harbor, but the air was clear and the weather to the advantage of the enemy. Guns began to thud, and shortly after they opened up, the bombs drifted swiftly downward on long and slanted courses to strike and strike again, and this time the damage was worse — much worse. A hanger crumpled. One wing of the hospital erupted upward in smoke and flame. The beached ship *Northwestern* was struck, and her portside forward was buckled in, revealing the roaring fires within the old hull. A moored PBY lifted up on a wave caused by a bomb explosion and sank down again, a broken thing.

Bob crouched on the deck of the *Otter,* unable to tear his gaze from those deadly silver gnats high in the morning sky. As he watched, one of them fell off on a wing and seemed to slide down a long and invisible wire toward the island with a stream of thin smoke staining the blue sky behind it.

There was an explosion ashore, followed by a dull thumping sound. Bob turned to look and saw one of the huge oil tanks belching out a ball of incandescent gas. The flames flicked toward another tank, and a moment later

15

it was flaring upward as well. Then, almost simultaneously both of the other tanks were hit and twenty-two thousand gallons of fuel oil roared upward in wild glee to spread a pall of heat and flame across the harbor through which guns spat flame and smoke toward the high-flying Japanese aircraft.

Another enemy bomber lost a wing and fell awkwardly, forming erratic spirals until the other wing sheared off and let the fuselage plunge javelinlike toward the ocean far below.

The gunfire never ceased, and shell fragments flicked up tiny spurts of water as they fell down into the harbor while bombs crumped and thudded along the shore near the burning *Northwestern*.

"We've got a charmed ship!" said Nels Andreason. "They can't hurt our little *Otter*!"

Even as he spoke, something struck just beyond the stern of the vessel and lifted her up as though in a gigantic but invisible hand, and where Nels Andreason had been standing was nothing but a pair of shoes, while fragments of the afterpart of the vessel rose upward like a fan of debris. Gary Lunt hit the deck. Mack Dunbar was hurled into a corner of the bridge. Something hit Bob with stunning force between the shoulder blades and smashed him to the deck. He lifted his head and dropped it, lifted it again and saw yellow tongues of flame licking up from the afterpart of the craft. She was adrift, wallowing gently as she headed for the shingle, feeling her way through the smoke toward the safety of the shore. Bob felt his senses reel and waver, lift high and fall, so that he seemed to plunge deeply into a bottomless abyss of the deepest black.

It seemed days later that he felt himself bobbing up and down, and for a moment he thought he was in the

16

harbor until he opened his eyes and saw the broad back of a man carrying the end of the stretcher at his feet. Bob was thickly covered in blankets and his naked upper body was swathed in thick bandages. He slowly turned his head.

" Take it easy, kid," said the man at the head end of the stretcher. " You got an awful hole in your back."

Bob swallowed hard and his head reeled. The last thing he saw, before he slid down into that awful abyss of nothingness once again, was the sight of *Otter* hard aground on the beach, with flames dancing and posturing about the smoke-shrouded after end of the stout hull and the upper structure. There was no doubt in his mind. *Otter* was evidently a total loss.

2

THE throbbing of the diesel exhaust came through the fog that enveloped Kodiak Harbor. It echoed back and forth from the warehouses and buildings along the shore.

"That'll likely be *Otter*," said a gnarled fisherman as he looked out into the fog. "You're lucky, kid. You might of waited days for her, or any other craft, in this fog."

Bob Dunbar nodded. He shifted his seabag from his shoulder and dropped it to the wharf. It was more than two months since he had seen his uncle's craft. In that time *Otter* had been chartered for Government work, and by the grapevine Bob had heard she was going to touch in at Kodiak on her way from Sitka back to Dutch. It had been swift work to say good-by to his quiet mother, take the Alaska Railway from Anchorage, where he had been convalescing at home, to Seward, where he had cadged a lift on the transport *Baranof* which had come into Kodiak the day before. It stayed only long enough to pick up some priority cargo and left again, destination unknown. Everything was hush-hush in Alaska and along the Aleutian Chain those days. The Japanese had occupied Attu and Kiska, at the far end of the chain, early in June, and from all reports they were there to stay, with submarines and surface craft to back them up, while the American forces felt about for them in the ever-present fog, like playing a deadly game of blindman's buff. There was a feeling of fear in Alaska, for long ago military experts had predicted that the Japanese might use the Aleutian Islands as vast stepping-stones to attack Alaska, and eventually the United States itself.

Bob eased his left shoulder. His wound was healed, but every so often it ached dully. The fragment of metal that had driven into his flesh had missed his spine by not more than an inch. If it had been a little more to the right, he would have died instantly on the deck of the *Otter* as Nels Andreason had done.

"Your Uncle Mack did a good job on repairing *Otter*," said the fisherman. He grinned. "The Navy boys at Dutch tried to tell him she was no good but for salvage, but they didn't know ol' Mack Dunbar. He borrowed, bought, and stole everything he needed to fix her up. Why, they tell me that some of the Army and Navy boys at Dutch, busy as they were themselves, used what little spare time they had to help him with the *Otter*."

Bob nodded. "The last I saw of her she was beached, broken, and afire," he said quietly.

"You can't wreck a boat like *Otter*," said the old man. His faded eyes looked out into the clinging fog. "It just ain't in the cards, especially when you got a skipper like Mack Dunbar. These are the toughest waters in the world, boy. I oughta know, I've seen most of 'em. Because they are the toughest waters in the world they breed the right men and the right ships for them. Look! There she is now!"

She appeared in an open space in the fog, and though Bob was sure it was the *Otter*, he wasn't quite ready for the changes in her appearance. No longer was she painted

19

black and white, with green trim. She was now colored a dirty-looking but concealing gray, and her trim pilothouse seemed bulkier. On her forward deck was something that looked like a light, shielded gun covered with weather-stained canvas. He could make out another gun much farther aft, on the rebuilt section of the craft.

As the *Otter* neared the wharf a man stepped up on the low forward deck with a heaving line in his hand and looked toward the wharf. The faint wind ruffled his ash-blond hair, and an eerie feeling crept over Bob. He stared at the man. No one else was visible on the *Otter* as she moved steadily toward the wharf — no one but the blond man, and that blond man was Nels Andreason, *or his ghost*. Bob knew well enough that Nels had been blown to bits at Dutch Harbor months ago.

The man drew back his arm and skillfully cast the heaving line toward the wharf. It struck Bob across the chest and fell to the wharf.

" Grab it, boy! " called out the fisherman. He stared at Bob's set white face, then snatched up the line and ran with it to haul in the heavier mooring line, which he passed swiftly about a bollard and made fast as *Otter* swung against the pilings and her motor was throttled down as she was put into neutral.

" You Bob Dunbar? " asked the man on the forward deck of the *Otter*.

Nothing but a dry croaking came from Bob's throat until he saw Gary Lunt running forward. " Bob! " he yelled. " We hoped you'd make it! Hop on board! We're shoving off right away! We're due at Dutch in the next few days." Gary stared at Bob. " What's wrong with you, pal? You look awful white. Maybe you're not ready to come back yet."

"Him," said Bob at last, pointing to the man on the forward deck.

"Oh, that's Thor Andreason, Nels's twin brother. He shipped on with us at Sitka. Came clean up from Seattle to ship on."

"Yeah?" croaked Bob. "That's nice."

Gary swung up onto the wharf, picked up Bob's seabag, and dropped back onto the deck of the *Otter*. "Come on," he said.

Bob went aboard. The bowline was cast off and *Otter* swung out into the harbor and moved slowly into the wreathing fog. Bob looked at Thor, and the resemblance to Nels was startling.

Thor smiled. "They've told me a lot about you, Bob," he said. He held out a hand and Bob gripped it. It was solid, muscular flesh. A picture came back to Bob across the miles of heaving waters between Kodiak and Dutch Harbor — a pair of empty shoes on the afterdeck of the *Otter*.

Thor picked up Bob's seabag. "You feeling all right now?" he asked.

"Yes."

"I know how you feel. I was at Pearl Harbor when the Japs hit it last December." He held up his left hand and Bob saw that it wasn't a hand of flesh and blood at all, but one of polished metal tubing and plastic. "Got a medical discharge," added Thor, "and was moping around Seattle when I heard your uncle was looking for hands. Well, *I've* got hands, even if one of them is made out of an Erector set. I can't fight on the old *Nevada* anymore, but I can do my bit on the *Otter*."

"It's good to have you aboard," said Bob quietly. "I've missed your brother, Thor."

21

The clear blue eyes studied Bob. "He thought a lot of you and your uncle," said Thor. He smiled. "Let's get a cup of joe!"

Bob climbed to the pilothouse first, and realized why it looked different. It had been encased in reinforced concrete for protection against fragments. His uncle's broad figure was framed in the door. He grinned and wrapped a thick arm about Bob's shoulders. "You all right, kid?" he asked gruffly.

"Shipshape and Bristol fashion," said Bob.

"Your mother all right?"

"Just fine."

"Your father?"

"Last thing we heard he was in Australia."

Mack nodded. "What do you think of *Otter?* The old girl has changed her dress, kid, but we can't expect her to wear a party frock when there's dirty work to do. We've even got a few guns to fight back with, Bob. Not much. A Navy twenty millimeter ... forward and a fifty caliber water-cooled Army machine gun aft, but at least we can make a noise, if nothing else. It won't be like it was at Dutch last June."

"What's doing out along the islands, Skipper?"

A veil of the fog seemed to float across Mack Dunbar's broad face. "Nothing much," he said.

"I see," said Bob. He did not press the issue, but there was an urgency about *Otter* this trip, in the steady thudding of her powerful diesel engine, the muted barking of her exhaust, the swashing of the seas back from her bluff bows. Something was in the wind. *Something* . . .

There were others aboard the *Otter,* as Bob learned in the mess. Baldy Barker still held sway in the galley, and of course there were Gary and Thor, but there were four

22

other men in the mess, two of them in Navy uniform and one in Army uniform, while the fourth man was a middle-aged civilian.

Baldy did the honors as he filled the coffee cups. Thor was on duty at the engine, while Mack conned the *Otter* out of the harbor, with Gary on lookout up forward.

"We'll introduce them in the order of their importance," said Baldy importantly. "The civvy is Jim Brannon, ex-Coast Guardsman, Bering Sea Patrol, now chief engineer aboard Otter. The tall, skinny guy in the swabbie's gear is Mike Pucci, chief gunner on the twenty millimeter up forward, and the chunky guy in the dirty whiskers is his assistant gunner, or whatever you call 'em, Homer Smith, better known as Smitty."

Bob shook hands all around, then looked at the sad-faced Army man, who was cuddling his lean hands about his thick coffee cup as though to warm them. "You forgot him," said Bob.

"Yeh," said Baldy. "Seems like I always do. That's Private Jesse L. Easter, sole representative of the Yewnited States Army aboard this bucket. Jesse *mans*, and I use the term loosely, the fifty caliber machine gun on the fantail."

Bob stared at the melancholy-looking soldier. "A soldier? Aboard the *Otter*?"

"Yup," said Baldy. "Seems like a small Army transport ran aground off Dutch. The crew was taken off, and as the transport had some Army antiaircraft gunners aboard for protection, they was transferred to one of the other transports that left for Seattle the same day. Somehow or another Jesse got left behind. No one seemed to know what to do with him."

"I'm whut they call a 'casual,' Robert," said Jesse in a mournful voice.

"Ain't no one more casual than Jesse L. Easter," said Mike Pucci in a decided Brooklyn accent. "Eh, Smitty?"

"Right," said Smitty.

Baldy shook his head. "We was heading for Sitka without any escort. They don't bother to escort craft like *Otter*, not that we *couldn't* handle a few Jap battlewagons, tin cans, and carriers singlehanded, in case they had the audacity to attack us."

"They only had one twenty millimeter gun to spare for the *Otter*," said Smitty, "but somebody scraped up a fifty caliber water-cooled machine gun from the Army."

"And, they scraped *Jesse* up with it," said Baldy.

"I'm whut they call a 'casual,' Robert," said Jesse.

He reminded Bob of nothing more than a sad-faced hound, hardly able to move except to scratch his fleas.

"There wasn't time to do anything about it," said Mike. "Jesse brought the gun aboard, but no one had told him to come back, so he stayed. He set it up and cleaned it and by that time we were out in Akutan Pass with Unalga Island to starboard."

"Too far to swim back," said Jesse tonelessly.

"Do they know he's aboard?" asked Bob. It was hard to keep a straight face.

"I suppose so," said Baldy. "Skipper sent a message back to Dutch while we were at Sitka. Couple of days later a message comes back."

"They never heard of me," said Jesse. He sipped his coffee and warmed his hands on the cup. "This is the coldest country I ever seen."

"This is August," said Bob. "Wait until October comes."

"And November and December," said Baldy. "Whoooeee!"

24

Jesse rolled his eyes upward. There was no need to speak.

"So the Skipper sent a message to Seattle before we left Sitka," said Smitty. "Figured the rest of his outfit was back there."

"We got a message back a few minutes before we left," said Mike.

"They never heard of me either," said Jesse.

"So now you know how we have Jesse L. Easter aboard," said Mike. "The Arkansas Traveler."

"I come from Tinsley, Arkansas," said Jesse.

"Where is that?" asked Bob.

"So fur up on the Ozarks yuh got to pipe sunshine up there, Robert," drawled Jesse. There wasn't the trace of a smile on his lean face.

Bob sipped his coffee. "Some ship," he said quietly. "Skippered by an ex-Navy CPO, with a one-handed veteran from Pearl, two high school kids from Anchorage, an ex-Coast Guardsman from the Bering Sea Patrol, an ex-chef from San Francisco in the galley, two gobs from the Navy, and a lost soul from the Army."

"I ain't exactly a lost soul, Robert," said Jesse mildly.

"I know," said Bob, trying to hide a grin, "you're a casual, Jesse."

"Yup, that's it."

Otter was lifting and falling to heavier seas now as she forged out of Chiniak Bay and met more open waters. Time for those off watch to turn in and those on watch to get about their duties. They'd need keen eyes and ears in that fog. Traveling alone, and so lightly armed, they'd be fair game for a Japanese submarine. Some of them, according to Baldy, had been reported by air patrols in that very area, and the waters off Dutch had known a number of them since the attacks by air in June.

Bob went back up on deck. *Otter* seemed none the worse for her damage sustained at Dutch Harbor, but she had been through rough experiences before in Aleutian and other waters. It was as the old fisherman at Kodiak had said. "You can't wreck a boat like *Otter*. It just ain't in the cards, especially when you got a skipper like Mack Dunbar."

It was getting dark now and *Otter* would practically have to smell her way through the islands as she headed for Dutch Harbor. Suddenly, to Bob Dunbar, the darkening waters seemed unutterably lonely. He was grateful for the shelter of the pilothouse, and at a nod from Mack Dunbar he took over the wheel, feeling the lift and sway of the sturdy boat as she rose to the swells. As heavily and solidly as she was built, there was a certain liveliness about *Otter* that was a peculiar feature of her own, as though she was a thing of life rather than a creation of wood and metal.

Mack filled his pipe and lighted it, eyeing Bob over the flare of the match. "Well," he asked quietly, "what do you think of the crew, kid?"

Bob smiled. "Some of them are a *little* different, Skipper."

Mack nodded. "They're a fair bunch. Even Jesse L. Easter."

"Him?"

"He's got his faults, but none of them are big ones, Bob. The Lord alone knows how he came to be aboard *Otter*, but I never question the ways of the Lord. He works in inscrutable ways. I always feel somehow, that each man has a hole to fit into, a hole that no other man can fill, and the time and place where he will fit that hole is not up to mortal man to predict."

"I always liked your optimism, Skipper."

Mack shrugged. "Call it what you will," he said quietly.

"What type of work are we doing, sir?"

Mack Dunbar laughed. "You name it; we do it. Ferry service men between the islands. A little salvage work. Carry freight. Supply remote outposts. Not much different, really, than what we've always done."

"Except we never did it in a shooting war."

Mack waved a hand. "It's been pretty quiet. Still, there are Jap subs in these waters. I always have a feeling one will rise up out of the water like a sea monster, dripping water, covered with slime, and ready to sink *Otter* as though she was a toy ship. *Otter* isn't rated high on the charter list, kid. We can't keep up with a fast convoy and can't carry enough freight or men to warrant being included in a convoy. They haven't got the ships to detail an escort for us, and the escorts are worth more than we are, anyway. So we plug along on the fringes of the war, almost forgotten, doing a job for which we seem peculiarly well fitted. No glory, but plenty of hard work. I know one thing —"

"Yes?"

"It's better than not being part of the big picture at all."

"Amen, Skipper."

Otter dipped deeply and sent up a shower of diamond-like spray. She rolled easily into the next wave. Homer Smith, whiskers flaring in the cold wind, made his way forward across the wet well deck and checked the lashings on the cover of the twenty millimeter gun.

Mack relighted his pipe. "You met those two swabbies from my forward gun crew, of course."

"Yes. I like them."

27

"Usually you get the leavings for gun crews on boats like this. Pucci, *chief gunner*, to gild the lily, and Smitty, must have been fugitives from a crew of galley slaves. Pucci intended to run *Otter*, and Smitty intended to have a glorious time doing absolutely nothing."

Bob glanced back at the hidden face of his uncle. He thought he knew what was coming. "Didn't they know about your Navy service, Skipper?"

"No."

Bob grinned widely. "But they know now, don't they?"

Mack drew in deeply on his pipe and the flaring up of the tobacco lighted his face. The eyes were set and hard. "They know now, kid," agreed Mack.

Bob wished he had seen the action that had taken place. Mike and Smitty must have caught a tartar that day.

"I'm not sure yet that they have the general idea," said Mack, "but the longer they serve aboard *Otter*, the more they'll learn."

They were well out of Chiniak Bay by now and the wind was picking up, rattling the shrouds, driving scud across the decks, feeling for the weak spots while *Otter*, like the veteran she was, snugged down and met anything the wind had to give, to let the elements know she knew her business too.

"How is the war going on out here?" asked Bob.

"Our subs have sunk a few of their ships. *Triton* sank a Jap tin can off Agattu. *Grunion* sank two subchasers and damaged a third off Kiska. Reported there was heavy Jap antisub activity off Kiska. That was the last ever heard of her. *Spurlos versenkt*, I'd say."

"What does that mean?"

"The Germans used that term in World War I. Sunk without trace. Our fly-boys — Navy and Army — have been

28

raiding Kiska as well as they can. The Navy is using PBY's, of all things. The sub tender *Gillis* is out there somewhere as a seaplane base. Jap Mavis flying boats attacked her, but did no damage. Our naval surface craft raided Kiska early this month. The rumor is that they sank a Jap transport of about eight thousand tons."

"Seems to me our forces ought to be moving out to meet the Japs instead of sitting back at Dutch, Cold Bay, and Umnak, waiting for them to come to *us*. We need bases farther along the chain, Skipper. Why don't we go out and get 'em?"

"Maybe we will, kid. *Maybe we will.*"

Bob turned to look at his uncle, but the face was as inscrutable as ever. Bob gathered that *Otter* was hurrying to Dutch Harbor, and this time it wouldn't be the same old hurry-up-and-wait business.

It was darker than ever by now. Gary Lunt came to the pilothouse. "Ships off the port beam, Skipper," he said.

"Ours?" asked Mack Dunbar.

"I'm not at all sure. Three transports, and possibly two four-pipe destroyers."

Mack grabbed his night glasses and walked out onto the little wing bridge. He steadied himself and studied the dim ships in the distance. Suddenly a signal lamp began to blink rapidly from one of the slim shapes — an old-fashioned flush-decked destroyer, with four funnels. The newer types were needed elsewhere, in the *shooting* war.

The destroyer's lamp was still blinking as she turned toward the low, dark shape of the *Otter*.

"Smitty!" called Mack Dunbar. "Get up here on the lamp! Flash the recognition signal!"

The transports and the other destroyer had turned away, while the first destroyer increased its speed.

"She's doing at least twenty knots," said Mack. "Smitty!"

There was no sign of the sailor. Mack ripped off the cover of the lamp, but something was wrong with the lamp switch. While he fumbled with it, the destroyer kept signaling. Bob swallowed hard and tried to keep his hands steady on the wheel spokes, but he was greasing them with cold sweat. Those destroyers took no chances.

"Smitty!" roared Mack Dunbar.

The bearded sailor came up from below, rubbing his eyes. He dashed to the lamp and worked at the switch. The lamp had just flicked on when something flashed on the forward deck of the tin can and an instant later came the roaring of a gun. Something rushed through the air ten feet above the pilothouse. It was excellent shooting from the deck of a pitching destroyer in the dark at such a small target.

Smitty's hands shook as he worked the lamp, frantically signaling the recognition code to the onrushing destroyer. The destroyer's lamp replied as she passed closer to the little, pitching *Otter*, veering off to steam at full speed back to join her charges and the other destroyer.

It was very quiet aboard the *Otter*. Every man was on deck. Sweat was running down Smitty's face and vanishing into his ragged beard as he covered the lamp. He did not dare look at Mack Dunbar.

"Ten feet lower, mister," said Mack quietly, "and that shell would have cleaned the pilothouse right off the deck of the *Otter*. Their next shot would have broken us in half, mister."

Smitty swallowed hard.

"Tighten up, mister," warned Mack Dunbar in a low, hard voice, "or you'll have the slack *taken* out of you."

Smitty flushed. "You can't talk to me like that," he said. "I'm in the *Navy*. You're only a civilian."

Mack tilted his head to one side and looked Smitty up and down. "*You?* In the *Navy?* I'm sick enough about what just happened without thinking you're in the Navy. Now get out of my sight!"

Smitty scuttled below.

Bob knew now what his uncle meant when he had spoken about the two Navy men aboard. Somewhere, sometime, within the weeks to come, Mack Dunbar would have to take *Otter* into the lonely and dangerous seas to the west, in a small vessel, inadequately armed, with boys, a cripple, casuals, and second-raters as her crew. The crew of a ship can make or break the ship. A tight crew makes a tight ship. When the chips are down is when the payoff comes, and Bob wasn't at all sure that the crew of the *Otter* could face up to the payoff when that time came — not in their present condition, at any rate.

His mood was as dark as the night and the fog as *Otter* slogged along through the rising seas, while the wind whistled dolefully through the rigging.

3

Rolling in the heavy swells, *Otter* lay a mile off the humped shape of Adak Island, part of the Andreanof group of the Aleutian Islands, while tendrils of fog drifted along the black sand beaches. Rising above the low-lying shore fog were the humped shapes of the mountains themselves, hung with drifting clouds. Below the dark mountains was the muskeg country, grass green, dotted with blue water lakes and ponds, and as naked of trees as an iceberg. *Otter* moved slowly along the foggy channel between Adak and the smaller island of Kagalaska, with three lookouts searching the forbidding shores with binoculars. Somewhere along those half-seen beaches, possibly in a rockbound cove or hidden harbor, a small supply barge had drifted ashore, lost from a tug tow several days before in a dense and clinging fog.

Bob Dunbar stood in the canvas-covered crow's nest almost at the top of the foremast, elbows resting on the rim of the crow's nest, while he searched those lonely shores for the lost barge. It was typical of the work they gave *Otter*. Not for her had been the little glory that had come to the force that had crept through the fog to land on Adak Island a few weeks ago, and the very tail end of the month of August. In ten days they had drained a flooded tidal basin, filled it, and were now finishing up the airfield, ready for the first strikes at Kiska. This was the first American air base in the Aleutians beyond Otter Point on Umnak Island almost four hundred miles to the east. Adak was about two hundred miles east of Kiska. Rumor had it that this would be the first of other such bases, leap-frogging the fog-shrouded islands to the west, along the far-flung sickle of the Aleutian Chain.

Otter had been ready to leave Dutch Harbor as part of a small auxiliary force of old destroyers, converted fishing craft, a Coast Guard patrol craft, and other odds and ends scraped together from Seattle to Dutch Harbor, to aid in the Adak landing, but she had instead been sent to Cold Bay to pick up some necessary equipment, and by the time she had returned to Dutch Harbor the landing had been effected and the airstrip was already started. She had been ordered to tow a small barge from Unalaska to Adak, which she had successfully done through comparatively calm seas. It was the same type of barge for which the crew of *Otter* was now looking. No other craft could be spared at that time for the job, and Bob thought that they had given *Otter* the task to keep her out of the way while more serious work was being done.

Bob glanced down at the pilothouse. His uncle was standing on the starboard wing bridge of the boat, hands thrust into his pea-coat pockets, unlighted pipe clenched in his mouth, jaw outthrust, and seagoing cap tilted far forward. Bob knew the storm signals, and he hoped some of the more careless of the crew of the *Otter* would recognize them as well. It wasn't the type of war duty Mack Dunbar wanted, but he'd do the job he was ordered to do.

There was no sight of the barge. Rain slanted suddenly down from gray clouds, stippling the greasy-looking swells. It had been raining off and on all that long day. There was nothing to indicate that a barge had struck any of those beaches — no wreckage, nothing at all to give the *Otter* a clue.

Bob looked back up the narrow waterway between the islands. They were getting quite a distance away from the harbor at Adak, and from the offshore patrols kept by the surface craft and PBY's. The United States forces didn't fully control those waters. Ships had been attacked by flying boats and floatplanes. Japanese subs were known to work close inshore looking for targets. An enemy sub had probed into Nazan Bay on Atka Island the day before American troops had landed on Adak and had slashed open the hull of the seaplane tender *Casco* with a torpedo, killing five men and wounding twenty. The *Casco* had somehow managed to limp back to Kodiak. The score wasn't all on the side of the Japanese, however, as a PBY had dropped a bomb near a submarine, starting an oil leak which had been trailed by the destroyer *Reid*. The *Reid* had dropped depth charges, forcing the sub to the surface, and had finished her off with gunfire. Only five of the submarine's crew had survived, or had *wanted* to survive. There was a difference among the fanatical Japanese. Most of them preferred *not* to surrender.

The rain slashed down harder, rattling against the decks and superstructure of the *Otter* like buckshot, and the shores of both islands vanished as though shrouded in gray cloth.

" Keep a sharp lookout up there! " snapped Mack Dunbar.

Bob jerked as his uncle's voice lashed at him. The charts issued for these waters were hardly as accurate as one would have wished. He tried to peer through the slanting rain. The glasses were of no help at all.

Otter's speed was reduced until she had only steerage-way, as Mack Dunbar felt his way through the rain and fog.

Bob turned to look to starboard, sweeping his eyes forward and then to port. He narrowed his eyes. Something was in the fog and rain several hundred yards from the boat, close to the shore of Kagalaska. Something that was manmade, for it was symmetrically shaped with straight and curved lines. The barge! " On the bridge! " he yelled down. " Barge! Dead off the port beam! Close inshore! "

He heard the engine-room telegraph ring. *Otter* stopped moving forward and began to drift toward the Kagalaska shore. The barge had vanished in the soup.

Otter drifted slowly, her engine barely turning over, but with no steerageway on her. She lifted easily on the swells and dropped again with a graceful motion. Waves lapped against her sides, surging up beneath her counter and bows with a sucking, gurgling sound.

Bob strained his eyes through the swirling, drifting fog. The rain died away as suddenly as it had come on. *Otter* rolled more heavily as she neared the unseen shore and the masts swung back and forth in erratic arcs. Bob's stomach churned uneasily.

"Up there! " snapped Mack Dunbar. "You sure you weren't seeing a phantom? "

Bob flushed. He had been quite sure at the time that he had seen something that looked like the barge, now he wasn't sure he had seen anything at all.

The wind shifted and began to scatter the clinging fog. Suddenly Bob saw a rock formation four or five hundred yards ahead appearing like a sea monster out of the fog. " Shore dead ahead! " he called down. " Four or five hundred yards! "

Mack Dunbar let *Otter* drift. He was standing at the front of the bridge, hands clamped on the rail, head tilted to one side, staring into the swirling opaqueness as though he hadn't heard.

Then Bob heard something throbbing faintly through the fog. It couldn't be waves washing against sand or rocks. There was only one sound like that. The exhaust of a diesel engine! At that instant Mack Dunbar rang to stop the engine. The throbbing of *Otter*'s diesel died away, and for a long moment Bob was sure he was hearing the echo of it, and suddenly the realization came to him that it was *not* an echo. There was another craft in that fog, and not too far away.

The fog swirled and lifted. Dead ahead, between *Otter* and the cold, forbidding rocks of the shore, was the low silhouette of a submarine, the hull barely awash, and the conning tower plainly seen against the darker rock. She wasn't two hundred yards ahead of the *Otter*. Bob stared at her. She wasn't an American fleet type sub, of that he was sure, for he knew them well, and besides, as far as he knew, all fleet type subs had been ordered out of those waters to more active theaters. It was an S boat. It had to be. The older and much smaller S boats had served in the Aleutians since the start of the war, and some of them were old enough to vote. It was about the size of an S boat, *but was it an S boat?*

"You asleep up there?" called Mack Dunbar.

Bob's throat went dry. Men had popped up on the deck of the strange submarine — small, bandy-legged men, wearing odd-looking caps. They were staring toward the place where the *Otter* was concealed in the fog, except for her foremast, which stuck up like a sore thumb, with a canvas-shielded crow's nest just below the top and within it a voiceless boy feeling like a clay pigeon, king size.

"Bob!" roared Mack Dunbar.

"Bob — Bob — Bob —" echoed the rocks along the shore.

Bob turned and leaned over as far as he could. He pointed. "Jap sub," he called. "Dead ahead! Two hundred yards!"

The fog parted and clearly in view was the submarine, with the gray seas washing over her hull. The little men were forming about a deck gun, training it toward *Otter*.

The engine-room telegraph rang. The motor throbbed into life. *Otter* surged forward, then swung wide, heading up the channel in the opposite direction from which the submarine was heading, while the gun crew hastily trained the gun as far around as they could. *Otter* headed toward a thick bank of fog.

Bob felt naked and alone up in his perch, but he could not leave his post, and besides, he could not take his eyes from that menacing gun behind the *Otter*. He could see Mack Dunbar's strategy now. He was heading in the opposite direction as swiftly as he could, keeping as close to the shore as possible, so that the gun crew could not train the gun far enough aft to get a sight on the boat. It would take time for the submarine to turn around, and *Otter* by that time might be safely concealed in the fog. The sub would have the legs on *Otter* in a surface chase, perhaps by four knots, and the gun could reach across the gap with efficient ease.

Otter swung away from the shore and fled like a live thing into the concealing and damp shelter of the fog. Bob looked ahead. There was something tossing up and down on the swells in mid-channel. The barge! She was heavily laden and seas were creaming across her rusty metal deck. " Barge! " called down Bob. " Dead ahead! Three hundred yards! "

For an instant Bob had the strange illusion that he was looking at some kind of naval craft, for aboard the barge, firmly lashed to the wet metal deck, were various types of earth-moving equipment, so necessary for the work at Adak. Several bulldozers and scrapers, some Athey carts, and towering above the barge, fore and aft, were a pair of steam shovels, with their shovel booms thrust up into the air like the masts of a ship. The fog swirled about the barge and *Otter* plowed on toward her at top speed.

Bob looked back. A patch of fog lifted and he saw that the submarine had turned about and was forging out into the channel, water washing over her low hull because of her speed. She was making fourteen to sixteen knots, full out. The gun crew clung to the gun, staring into the swirling fog, gunpointers with eyes glued to their sights. One clear shot and *Otter* would go straight to the bottom of the icy seas.

At a signal from Mack Dunbar, Thor Andreason, who was at the helm, put her hard over. *Otter* leaned sickeningly and Bob thought he would be pitched headfirst out of the crow's nest into the cold, gray waters. The boat shot past the rusty stern of the barge, with inches to spare, then, at another signal from Mack, *Otter* turned again, keeping the heavily laden barge between her and the submarine.

Mike Pucci and Smitty raced forward and were tugging at the canvas cover of the twenty millimeter gun. Jesse Easter stood at the after rail of the boat, hands gripping the railing, staring back into the fog, his fifty caliber

38

gun still swathed in its cover.

Mike stripped the cover from the gun and Smitty yanked down on the cocking rope to cock the quick-firing gun. Mike swung the gun about, aiming it across the bulwark in the general direction of the submarine. " Just give me one shot at them Nips! " he roared belligerently.

Mack leaned forward. " Get away from that gun, you crazy fool! " he yelled.

" You want to give up, hey? " snarled Mike.

" Get away from that gun! "

" We're Navy! We got to protect this boat! "

" You won't protect it by shooting that popgun! "

" That's up to *me* to decide! "

Mack Dunbar spoke over his shoulder to Thor and then slid down the ladder, crossing the well deck with short, plunging strides. Mike stepped away from the gun. He raised his fists. Smitty picked up a billet of wood from the deck. Gary Lunt started toward the smaller of the two sailors. It wasn't necessary. Mike made one pass at Mack and got an oak-hard left fist into his stomach. His down-coming chin met an upcoming right fist, snapping back his head. He hit the shield of the gun and fell heavily. Smitty swung at Mack. Mack's left hand came up, grip-ping Smitty's wrist, twisting it hard. A knee came up into Smitty's stomach and a right hook chopped at his jaw, just once, flattening the whiskers and Smitty as well. Mack turned on a heel and ran back toward the bridge.

Somewhere astern of the *Otter* a gun flatted off in the swirling fog and a moment later something rushed through the air, high over the barge and the *Otter*. At that instant *Otter* heeled sharp to starboard, throwing Gary Lunt into the scuppers where Mike Pucci and Smitty rolled over on top of him, while *Otter* took a deep, cold drink of the water over her starboard bulwarks, flowing it a foot deep over the three of them.

Bob had nearly been hurled from the crow's nest. Mack Dunbar darted into the pilothouse, and a moment later thrust his head through a window. " Bob! Come down and take the helm! " His head vanished.

Bob wasn't loathe to leave the exposed crow's nest. He scuttled down the port ratlines and ran aft to the port ladder, ran up it and into the pilothouse. Thor sat in a corner, his back to the wall, with his hands — both flesh and mechanical — covering his face. His shoulders shook and a dry sobbing sound came from him.

" Take the helm, Bob! " snapped Mack. " Hard aport! "

Bob gripped the spokes and spun the wheel. *Otter* heeled over again, this time rolling Gary, Mike, and Smitty clear across the deck to the port waterways, where once again *Otter* covered them with cold water. The three of them were spluttering and yelling. Bob couldn't help grinning, despite his fear. There was a faint yelling sound from aft that drifted off into the fog.

The fog cleared a little. Once again the Japanese gun flatted off and the rushing sound came again, but this time the *Otter* wasn't the target. She was firing, for some loco reason or another, at the barge now far astern and to starboard of the *Otter*, almost in mid-channel.

As *Otter* kept turning full circle Bob saw the submarine come into view, but it looked different, for the gun crew had vanished. There was no one on the small bridge. The sub was slanting forward down under the waves in a crash dive, and even as Bob watched she vanished, leaving a swirling wake of bubbles and white water behind her on the surface of the channel.

Mack Dunbar rang for half speed. " Turn back toward

40

the barge," he said to Bob.

Bob stared at him. "Maybe we ought to hightail it out of here," he said. He winced as he saw the look in his uncle's eyes.

"We came out here for that barge," said Mack flatly. "We're taking it back to Adak."

Bob returned to his job with a distinct impression that it was better to go back for the barge, risking a torpedo from the vanished submarine, than to have to face that look on his uncle's face.

"You swabs get up off my clean decks! " roared Mack Dunbar at the three soaked crewmen on the foredeck. "Get the cover on that gun! Gary! Get out the towing hawser! Mike, you give him a hand! "

Otter forged slowly toward the barge. They came gently alongside and Gary leaped aboard the barge, hauling a light line to which was attached a heavier line, and then the hawser itself was snaked, dripping, aboard and made fast to the towing bitts of the barge. Gary leaped back aboard *Otter* and the boat moved down channel very slowly, taking up the slack in the towing hawser. A heavy sea made the *Otter* dip, and as she arose the hawser straightened out, spurting water jets from between the strands. *Otter* shuddered from forefoot to counter as she took up the strain.

They'd hardly make three or four knots towing that lump of metal back there, and the submarine could slip a tin fish into them with ease, or even surface and sink them with the deck gun. He glanced at his uncle. Mack Dunbar was looking out of a window, watching the barge astern of them. "Ease the helm a little to port," he said over his shoulder. He rang for still slower speed.

It was starting to get dark. Rain slanted down again through the swirling fog. Now and then *Otter* dipped

41

deeply, thrusting her bows deep into the gray seas, filling her well deck with gray water from bulwark to bulwark, shaking herself like a wet dog as she came up again to face the next heavy sea, and the next, and the next. . . . It was going to be a long night indeed.

Thor Andreason stood up. His face was white and set. "I'm sorry, Skipper," he said quietly. "I went to pieces when I heard that Jap gun. I thought I was all over that kind of feeling."

"Forget it, Thor," said the skipper.

"I nearly swamped *Otter*, Skipper. I thought I was all right. They told me I was all right before they released me from the hospital."

"Forget it."

Thor wiped the sweat from his face. "I'll leave *Otter* at Adak," he said.

Mack whirled. "No you won't! You'll stay aboard and do your job! You *signed* aboard. You'll *stay* aboard. Now get below and see that Baldy gets a bucket of joe made. It's going to be a long, cold night out here. Jump!"

When Thor was gone, Mack came to stand beside Bob. "I've seen that happen before," he said quietly.

"You were pretty rough on him."

"How do you think I felt when he panicked at the helm? The lives of other men, as well as the life of *Otter*, were in his hands. Another thing, kid, if Mike had fired that popgun at that submarine, they would have hunted us down like rats. They'd have sunk us with one round and let us die in these waters."

Bob eyed his uncle. "You really can't blame anyone for getting rattled, Skipper."

Mack shook his head. He filled his pipe and grinned. "Those Nips must have thought that barge, with those pieces of equipment sticking up, was an antisubmarine vessel. Did you see them crash dive as though the devil was after them? "

" Is that why you headed for the barge? "

Mack lighted his pipe. " You're getting the idea, kid. Ease the helm a little."

It was difficult to keep the *Otter* heading into the waves with the dead, sluggish weight of the barge far behind them, half hidden in the fog, wallowing up and down, yawing from side to side, fighting the hawser like an insensate thing.

Gary Lunt came into the pilothouse with a coffeepot and cups. He placed them in the little fiddle board fitted to a shelf at the side of the structure. He looked at Mack. " Jesse Easter is missing, Skipper," he said quietly.

" You're sure? " demanded Mack.

Gary nodded. " We've hunted high and low for him, sir."

Something came back to Bob. When his uncle had commanded him to turn the helm hard aport and *Otter* had heeled heavily in response to her helm, Bob had heard a faint yelling sound from aft that seemingly had drifted off into the concealing fog.

Otter lifted and plunged, lifted and plunged, fighting to keep steerageway on that mass of metal dragging far astern. A sea was making up in the channel. A sea that would form into a cross sea because of the shape of the shorelines. Seas that would wrack at the vessel from both sides, making heavy work for so light a vessel.

" You're absolutely sure he's not aboard, Gary? " asked Mack quietly.

" Positive, sir."

Bob told them of what he suspected. It must have been the voice of Jesse calling through the fog. Calling for help. Calling for help that would not come. A man lived for about twelve minutes in those waters.

4

In the watery light of dawn *Otter* moved slowly into the open harbor of Adak after being passed by the patrol vessel at the harbor's mouth. They say a machine, or a ship, *can't* get tired. They wear out or lose power, but they don't get tired, although *Otter* seemed tired that cold morning.

Bob Dunbar stood at the after rail of *Otter* watching the barge towed astern. The harbor waters were comparatively calm after the passage of the night. The moored vessels rolled easily. Ashore, trucks moved and bulldozers roared steadily, for duty was twenty-four hours a day for all units ashore, with twelve-hour shifts to some extent, seven days a week. Cargo was being unloaded from ships in the harbor into the barges, while barges at the shore were being emptied into trucks and Athey carts for disposal in the growing, spreading supply dumps scattered over acres beyond the shoreline.

A PBY gathered speed, roaring across the choppy waters, to lift slowly into the gray light of the morning, then turn slowly to the north for the beginning of a long and dangerous patrol. The big Cats were slow and unwieldy, hardly a match for the lighter, swifter Japanese floatplanes they might encounter to the west, but they could fly in weather that would sock in any other kind of plane.

A powerboat foamed alongside *Otter*. "Anchor that

barge about two hundred yards offshore dead ahead, Skipper. Excellent work!" called out the naval officer in the boat.

Otter slowed down a little. The barge began to surge forward, and by the time *Otter* had lost way the barge was close alongside. Bob jumped onto her wet deck and stood by the bitts, ready to cast off. Heavy anchors hung at each side of the barge's squared-off bows, ready to be released by tripping a chain slip stopper. At a signal from Mack Dunbar, Bob released the towing hawser and let fall one of the barge's anchors. She drifted until the anchor caught hold, then rounded into the wind. As she did so, Bob let fall the second anchor. It plunged into the cold waters and as the strain came on the cable, the barge shuddered and swung easily up and down on the waves.

Bob waited for *Otter* to come alongside and pick him up. He was glad to get rid of the barge. He hated the feeling of her rusty plates beneath his feet.

Something grated not far behind him. "What time is chow, Robert?" a plaintive voice asked. "A man cud die of cold in this country."

Bob whirled to see the thin face of Jesse L. Easter peering at him from the open door of one of the cabbed bulldozers. "How'd you get here, Jesse?" demanded Bob.

Jesse grinned shamefacedly. "Fell plumb overboard when the ol' *Otter* did them didoes. Figgered I'd better get aboard this here barge to get warm. Didn' get a chance to yell out or anythin' when yuh boys hooked up to her. So, I made myself to home in here. Weren't bad, Robert, ceptin' there ain't no heat, and no galley aboard. You say they got chow aboard? Some of them powdered eggs maybe, or a bowl of that good mush ol' Baldy makes up?"

45

Bob's eyes watered in the cold wind. He looked quickly away. "Yeh, Jesse," he said quietly. "You can eat out the whole galley if you like."

Once they were on board *Otter*, Jesse almost did clean out the galley. It was amazing how the lean Arkansas boy could eat.

Bob talked to his uncle in the skipper's little cabin later that day. "Do you plan to get rid of Mike, Smitty, Thor, and Jesse while we're here?"

Mack relighted his pipe. "I can't get anyone to replace them, Bob. I thought they'd take Jesse back, but no one seems to know what to do with him other than to put him to work out in the mud and the cold."

Bob eyed his uncle, looking for a glint of pity in those steely eyes. "How hard did you try?" he asked.

Mack shrugged. "I wouldn't put a hound to work on these godforsaken islands," he said gruffly.

"There are a lot of men working on this one just the same, Skipper."

Mack puffed at his pipe. "Jesse is only another back and pair of hands to put to work. I don't think it makes any difference to them whether or not he's working ashore or on *Otter*, do you?"

"No, sir." Bob walked to the door. He looked back. "At least Jesse had enough sense not to try to shoot like Mike and Smitty did."

"Yeh. On the other hand, maybe he couldn't think as fast as they could either."

"What do we do next, sir?"

"Who knows? *Otter* took a beating yesterday and last night, kid. She's tough and knows her business, but too much of that and she won't be worth a plugged nickel. It's getting to be a hard war out here, kid, and I don't mean just against the Japs."

Later, as Bob was up on the deck watching the many shore activities, he thought of *Otter*. Bigger and tougher ships than *Otter* had succumbed to those dangerous seas. Mack Dunbar wouldn't give in, nor would *Otter*. War is sacrifice, for ships as well as men.

The faint humming of airplane engines came to him as he stood there on the deck. He turned to see low-flying planes heading for the new airfield on Adak. Big-bellied Liberators, the powerful and long-range B-24 heavy bombers, were flying into Adak escorted by the waspish-looking, twin-engined, twin-boomed Lightnings, the P-38 long-range fighter planes. Things were looking up for the American forces in the Aleutians, but there was another enemy beyond the hard-fighting and tenacious Japanese. A tougher enemy, who had controlled those far-flung islands before the time of man. His name was Weather. The Aleutians breed foul weather as no other place in the world does. It was early September, and by November King Weather would be in full sway again over his lonely domain.

In a sense, the Aleutians are a world still in the making. Amidst the fogs and sudden storms volcanoes blow mysterious rings of steam and smoke. Islets pop out of the water, stay a while, then vanish as suddenly as they appear. The stable islands are wild and inhospitable, shaken every now and then by earthquakes and wracked by savage williwaws, or the taku — the wind that blows with solid and unrelenting fury for two or three days and boxes the compass in the process.

The islands are deceptively green, looking like lush pastures, but a cow would starve to death on them. The Aleutians are wrapped in almost perpetual fog because of the cold water and air of the Bering Sea meeting the warm Japan Current of the North Pacific. Rain beats the islands for as many as two hundred and fifty days a year, soaking into the viscuous mud that lies just beneath the spongy mat of grasses called tundra, and forming unseen traps for the unwary. To make airfields and roads, this thick and spongy layer of grass and mud must be stripped off by bulldozer to a depth of as many as ten or fifteen feet to find the hardpan beneath. Tents and buildings have to be dug in, or the howling winter winds will sweep them clean from the spongy ground.

All the islands are mountainous, for they are indeed the tops of submerged mountains thrusting themselves up into the lonely, foggy seas. There is little animal life on them other than birds and foxes. There are few places level enough for airfields and few harbors safe enough for large ships. There is the fog and the rain in the summer, socking in the airfields, and making navigation by air or sea difficult, if not impossible. There are the howling winds and slashing icy rains and snows of the winter, the heaving seas, pale green and gray liquid mountains rising and falling, up which laboriously climb the ships, only to slide down the other side with a rush, as though to bury themselves forever, only to lift and shudder, to meet the next savage rush of wind and water, and sometimes they do *not* come up.

Bob paced back and forth on the deck, watching the bombers and fighters come in one by one, feeling their way down upon the metal stripping laid upon the airfield, to land with a clattering sound. Already the soldiers, airmen, and sailors who served in the Aleutians considered such duty as little more than penal servitude. There would be little fame or fortune in this campaign; nothing but boredom between fighting the weather, and the Japs, when they showed up.

48

Gary Lunt came up on deck beside Bob and leaned against the bulwark. He handed Bob a freshly made doughnut, coated with sugar. "Baldy outdid himself. I told him we could have used these for anchors on that blasted barge. I'm lucky I got out of the galley ahead of his cleaver."

Bob sank his teeth into the delicacy. "How is it below?"

"Meaning?"

"The jolly crew of the *Otter*."

Gary nearly choked on his doughnut. "Man, oh man! When those two swabbies were going to give your Uncle Mack a hard time about shooting that twenty millimeter I had an idea they didn't know ol' Barnacle Bill very well. They do now. Mike says he's going ashore to put in a complaint. Baldy says if he does, he, Baldy, will take up where the skipper left off. So Smitty got smart with Baldy and it took Thor and me to get the two of them apart."

"You think they'll report him?" asked Bob soberly.

Gary flipped a piece of doughnut toward a squawking gull. "Naw! They know he was right. Besides, you know very well those two characters don't want to serve on a real Navy ship if they can get out of it. A tough bos'n's mate would be rougher on those two characters than your uncle was."

"The whole thing was pretty close, Gary. Too close to suit me. We're lucky we got out of that mess alive."

"Yep. I think everyone aboard, with the exception of Mike and Smitty, agree that your uncle saved us and the *Otter* by his tactics. If Mike had started shooting . . . I hate to think of it. Your uncle is holding this crew together by sheer nerve most of the time. What happened to Thor?"

"Nothing." Bob looked away.

"He got chicken up there, didn't he? I'm not blaming him, pal, but these waters are no place for a man who has lost his nerve."

"How would you feel if you had lost a hand at Pearl?"

"That's not the point! You know it as well as I do. We both thought a lot of Nels and I want to think a lot of Thor, but, man oh man, if he pulls a stunt like that again!"

Bob nodded, as much as he hated to. Gary was right. Aleutian waters, even in times of peace, were no place for a man whose nerves were shot.

"Your uncle going to keep Thor aboard?" asked Gary.

"As far as I know."

"That's all we need! Two mutinous swabbies, an Arkansas hillbilly who can't keep his feet on a deck, and a one-handed man who goes haywire!"

Bob sensed someone behind him. He turned slowly. Thor Andreason was standing at the foot of the port ladder, his metal hand hooked over one of the steps, staring at the two boys with a taut, white face.

Gary flushed. He held out a hand. "I'm sorry, Thor," he said quietly. "I've got a big mouth."

For a long moment the maimed veteran stood there, then he smiled a little, but there was no smile in his blue eyes. "It's all right, kid," he said softly. "Don't ever apologize for the naked truth, no matter how much it hurts a man." He turned on a heel and entered a door that led into the quarters aft of the little well deck.

Bob looked up to see his uncle standing on the starboard wing of the little bridge, looking down at the two boys. "Gary didn't mean it, Skipper," he said.

Mack Dunbar took his pipe from his mouth. "Yes, he did," he said. "He'll have to make it up to that man one way or another. Remember this, boys, this is a small ship,

50

and the human voice has a nasty way of carrying farther than most people think it does. Thor slipped, out there in the channel, but I've seen men who aren't carrying his burden slip up worse than that. Don't forget it. We owe it to Thor, and Nels as well, to help him as much as we can. I'm game to try it. Are you?"

Both boys nodded. Mack Dunbar walked into the pilot-house.

"I feel like a born idiot," said Gary.

"You ought to," said Bob, "because you *are*."

"O.K.," said Gary.

As the pale darkness grew about the island and the shore lights flicked on, the wind began to rise, moaning over the island with a dirgelike quality.

"It won't be long before the winter storms start," said Gary thoughtfully. "You think they'll keep us out here?"

"I suppose so."

"Your uncle could pull a few strings and get us sent back. *Otter* is a little small for the kind of work they expect out of us."

"There's a war on, pal," said Bob.

Gary nodded. "Wishful thinking, I guess. I'll stay with *Otter* no matter where she goes or what she does."

There wasn't much conversation at the mess table that night, nor later when a fuel barge came alongside and topped the *Otter's* tanks with dark diesel fuel oil. Later on that night *Otter* left her mooring and headed out to sea, blinker lamp flicking out recognition signals to the lean and watchful destroyer that flitted through the darkness offshore. Mack Dunbar passed the word along that a Navy patrol torpedo boat had gone aground on its way to Adak and that the crew had been taken off by one of the other boats in the squadron. The boat was supposed to be a total loss, but Mack Dunbar had been ordered to take a look at it, and save it if he could. She had taken the bottom in an isolated cove on the dangerous northern shore of big Atka Island, a good seventy-five miles east of Adak.

Otter was snugged down for sea when she cleared the coast of Adak. It was rough, and storm warnings had been sent to all ships at sea in that area. It was nothing worse than *Otter* had experienced before many times in those waters. As long as she kept out to sea there was little danger, but if she had to approach the dangerous Atka coast the next day to look for the PT boat, the peril would be great.

Bob was at the wheel as *Otter* plunged into the roughening waters. *Otter* rolled easily and gracefully like the old professional she was. There was little light in the pilot-house other than the hooded binnacle light shining on the compass. Mack Dunbar paced back and forth. Up forward on the deck, clinging to the twenty millimeter gun, was Gary Lunt, swathed in parka and oilskins, trying to keep a lookout through the stinging salt spray and the shrouding darkness.

The throbbing of the diesel sounded through the night, mingled with the moaning of the night wind and the heavy swashing of the waves alongside the sturdy hull of the boat. Deep, deep went the bows, and green-gray water surged up over them to flow aft, flooding the well deck. *Otter* shook herself a little and arose, with streams of water pouring from the scuppers and freeing ports. She shuddered a little, then plunged deeply again, rolling slowly from side to side as she fought the rising seas.

Mack Dunbar bent over his chart table, lighted by a shielded lamp, and studied the chart. The wind had been coming from the northeast and now it was moving more to the north. The scend of the sea was changing and the movement of the boat indicated it. They had to pass south of the grouped islands of Great Sitkin, Igitkin, Chugal, and Tagalak, then turn up the pass to make a landfall on Cape Kigun at the very tip of Atka Island. East along the northern coast of Atka was the cove where the PT boat was supposed to be. The changing of the wind would set great seas battering against that coast.

Bob watched his uncle. No man likes to take his ship into such waters, and *Otter* was such a little ship. Hanging on the bulkhead was a little printed card. Bob knew the text by heart. *O Lord, watch over me, for the sea is so large and my ship is so small.*

Otter shuddered again and again as she plowed into the heavier seas. The skipper rang for less speed, testing *Otter* until at last she seemed to have the right combination of speed and angle into the seas.

Somewhere below something broke loose and clattered across the deck. A door slammed within the superstructure. Bob bent his knees to ride with the pitching deck as he steered the vessel into the rising blow. A coffee cup leaped out of the little fiddle board on the shelf and smashed against the deck.

Mack came over to take the wheel. "Tell that boy to come in off that deck. I can't have him take a chance in these seas. He can watch from the bridge wing. Go down and get a pot of joe after you bring Gary back. It's going to be a long night, kid."

Bob made his way forward. The well deck was knee-deep in icy seawater. He beckoned to Gary. Gary started aft, and as he did so the *Otter* dived deeply and water flowed two feet deep over her bows. Bob yelled. The two boys raced aft, but the water was too fast for them. By

53

the time it reached them it was four feet deep, and they ended up against the forward end of the superstructure, with the flood completely over them. The door behind them was smashed open and they and the water poured into the superstructure, clear to the after end, beside the galley door. A foot of water surged to and fro, looking for an outlet. Thor Andreason opened an after door and let the water out, while Jim Brannon slammed shut the forward door in the very face of another wave and braced it shut with some wooden bars.

The action of the boat seemed worse below than it was on deck. The deck was a litter of broken crockery, soaked clothing, wet food, and other odds and ends. Bob worked his way toward the ladder that led up into the pilothouse from the forward end of the superstructure. As he passed the sleeping quarters he heard a groaning sound from within. He peered inside and saw Mike Pucci propped in his bunk reading a soft-cover novel. Smitty was sound asleep. It was Jesse L. Easter who was making the groaning noise. He lay flat in his bunk, wedged in by his lifebelt, steel helmet, and a roll of blankets. His eyes were wide in his head and his face was a pasty green.

"He's like to dying," said Mike casually. He turned a page. "Never seen a fella so sick in my life before. This baby is rolling like a tin can."

Jesse groaned. "Shoot me," he gasped. "Throw me ovah the side. I can't live the night out, Robert."

Bob shook his head in sympathy. "This is just a little blow, Jesse."

Jesse turned his tortured face to the wall. "I wisht I'd never left Arkansas," he croaked.

Bob swiftly changed to dry clothing, got coffeepot and cups from the galley, then joined Mack Dunbar and Gary in the pilothouse. Gary was now at the wheel and Bob glued his face to one of the windows, trying to see through the flying spray and the darkness. No one could stay on that forward deck, and the wind was roaring across the tip-tilted seas in a wild frenzy, driving diamond-hard spray ahead of it.

"How is it below?" asked Mack.

"Rough, Skipper," said Bob.

"We can't run away from this storm. We've got to keep plugging on. I want to be off Cape Kigun by dawn for a fix."

Gary glanced at Bob, and Bob knew what his partner was thinking. With that sea and that wind, on a passage as dark as the inside of a seaboot, a man would have to be a wizard to hit the Cape Kigun area by dawn. If he missed, one way or the other, the *Otter* could hit unseen rock beneath the surface, or be driven on a lee shore, and if she was, there'd be no time to get the small boats into the water.

As the dark night wore on, the storm became worse, tearing at the water and the vessel with insensate fury, rending and trying to destroy completely. There could be no sleep on Otter that night, for no man could stay in a bunk, and even if he could, the slamming about of the boat would not allow him any rest.

Again and again *Otter* would dive deeply, as though she'd never come up, then she'd shudder a little, shake herself, and rise to the occasion, crawling up the icy slopes at lowest possible speed, racking and groaning in every timber, with solid water filling her decks and smashing everything in sight, tearing loose everything that was not triply secured.

It was a weary Bob Dunbar who stood his trick at the

wheel, watching the compass, never taking his eyes from it to look up at the black rectangles of the windows streaming with rain and spray. His uncle stood to one side, not far from the chart table, eyes half closed, big hands holding to a handrail. Gary sat in a chair that was bolted to the deck, hanging on to a handrail, feet hooked beneath a chair rung, head lolling back and forth, trying the impossible — that is, to sleep.

Bob had no idea how many hours they had fought the madness of the storm. His eyes burned and his muscles were sore from fighting the wheel. His feet and calf muscles ached dully. He looked up and was startled, for it seemed to him the windows were lighter. He realized it was the faint, watery light of the coming dawn.

Otter plunged down and then slowly came up again. As she arose, Bob saw something through the flying spume and rain — a dark, almost invisible and shapeless mass two points off the port bow. He stared at it and opened his mouth.

Mack Dunbar opened his eyes. " Cape Kigun," he said quietly. " I'll take the helm, Bob. You and Gary go below. You can get some sleep while we find the PT boat. Send Mike Pucci up to take the helm."

Bob waited for Gary at the bottom of the ladder. Gary had a look of wonderment on his face. " It's impossible," he said. " We spotted Cape Kigun just at dawn. Another hour of darkness and we might have found the cape by hitting it. I still don't believe it. How does he do it? "

Bob shrugged. " Smells the land," he said. " One thing I do know: I'm glad he was doing the navigating."

Otter seemed to shake herself as though in agreement, but then she had known all along that Mack Dunbar wasn't about to let *her* pile up on Cape Kigun.

56

5

THE bitter wind was mouthing in full force from the north, driving the gray-green seas ahead of it with raging fury, smashing them on the naked beaches and towering them in sheets and sprays of spume and froth against the dark rocky areas of the Atka shoreline. The lowering sky was thick with racing clouds. There was a mournful, dirge-like quality in the voice of the mad wind.

Otter plunged in through the whirlpool at the mouth of the cove, not fifty yards from a sheer wall of black rock, creamed with the washing of the great seas, while Gary Lunt hung on to the forestay with an arm hooked about it, casting the lead like an expert as the craft inched into the dubious shelter of the cove. Bob was on the starboard wing bridge, looking down into the heaving waters for telltale signs of rocks just below the surface, while Smitty hung on to the railing of the port wing bridge doing the same duty.

Mike Pucci was up forward, ready to trip the anchor at the right instant. Even Baldy, the cook, was on deck, peering nearsightedly at the inhospitable waters and shoreline of the cove. On the little afterdeck, out of sight, was Thor Andreason ready to cut loose the stern kedge anchor at a signal if anything went wrong. Jim Brannon was at the engine, and Jesse Easter was lying helplessly in his bunk, still a victim of seasickness.

A great wave surged through the cove entrance, driving *Otter* forward. " By the mark five! " called out Gary. " By the mark four and a half! By the mark four underwater! Shoaling fast, sir! "

Mack Dunbar nodded. He steered closer to the sheer rocky walls to starboard of *Otter*.

" Rocks underwater off the port bow! " called Smitty.

" I can see bottom thirty feet to starboard. Rocky," said Bob.

" By the mark three! " chanted Gary. Eighteen feet depth under the bows of *Otter*. She had ten feet and six inches maximum draft.

The PT boat lay battered in the surf, stern in the water, rising and falling, while the sleek bows ground against shattered rocks and driftwood beneath a sheer bluff. She was a good three hundred yards within the narrowing walls of the cove.

" By the mark three and a half! " called out Gary. " By the mark four underwater! By the mark four and a half! "

Mack Dunbar rang for slow speed. *Otter* moved slowly past the sheer rock wall on the starboard, with the shoal of rocks not ten feet from her wooden side. Mike Pucci glanced nervously up at the pilothouse.

" By the mark four! " called Gary. " By the mark three and a half! By the mark three underwater! "

Otter inched along. Mack swung the wheel a little and angled back toward the middle of the cove.

" By the mark two and a half underwater! " chanted Gary.

Mack rang for reverse. " Let go the bow anchor! " he called.

Mike tripped the cable and the anchor plunged into the

58

water. The reversing of the motor dragged the anchor deep into the bottom, setting the flukes. " Let go stern anchor! " called Mack. Thor dropped the kedge. *Otter* was moved forward a little, then she seemed to settle down, riding easily at her two anchors. Mack rang for Finished with Engine, and walked out onto the wing bridge beside Bob. He eyed the PT boat. " Even if we can get her afloat," he said, " it won't be a cinch towing her out of here. She's a heavy craft, kid."

" You didn't have to agree to save her, Skipper," said Bob.

Mack filled his pipe. " I said I'd bring her back if it was at all possible," he said. " We need every boat we can get out here. Get the powerboat into the water. You and Gary can crew. Tell Jim Brannon I want him to go along."

They lowered the starboard boat into the water. Jim Brannon handed down some tools to the boys and got into the boat. Mack Dunbar took the helm and steered for the shore at a slow rate of speed while Bob and Gary watched for rocks. They eased into the shallow surf, and Bob slipped over the side to take a mooring line ashore. The others heaved the boat up higher on the dark sands, and walked with Bob toward the stranded hull of the PT boat.

Mack whistled softly as he saw the starboard bow. A great ragged hole had been punched through the thick plywood. He looked at Jim. " Can we patch that, Jim? "

Jim shrugged. " We've got some marine plywood aboard," he said. He looked out toward the mouth of the cove. " It'll be another thing pulling her off, and once we get out to sea that patch'll take a beating."

They swarmed aboard the wrecked craft. Anything that could be removed had been taken away by the boats that had rescued the crew. The motors were still in good condition and the tanks had fuel in them. Water flowed in and out of the hull through the hole in the bow. The boat was about seventy feet long, with three powerful gas engines, and Bob had heard the PT's could do about fifty knots full out.

Mack Dunbar waded about the hole in the bow. "She weighs about fifty tons," he said, half to himself. "Not hard to tow, either. We might get the engines going."

Gary peered through the hole from the outside of the hull. "Two of her props are useless," he said. "The other one is a little bent but looks as if it might be all right if we have to use it."

"Great," said Mack. "I was wondering how we'd get her out into the deeper water. What about the hole, Jim?"

"We can drill holes through the plywood, all around the hole, fit a piece of plywood outside, fill the space between it and another slab of plywood with calking, or something, then bolt the two together through the hull itself, like a wood sandwich. That should keep the water out unless a seam has split somewhere. We can't figure that out until we get the water out of her."

"Yeh," said Mack. "Besides, this water makes the hull too heavy for us to get her afloat again. Let's get started."

Rain pattered down as Jim began to drill holes through the tough marine plywood. Bob and Gary went back to *Otter* for plywood, bolts, calking, and other odds and ends. They brought back oilskins for the others. The rain came down steadily, forming an opaque mist that cut off their view of the sea. Bob had the uncomfortable feeling that if a Japanese submarine poked its nose in there, they'd have *Otter* like a frog in a bottle.

All that day and night the crew worked in shifts patching the hull, while heavier and heavier seas battered at the coastline, showering spray and spume high into the air, driving masses of icy water high over the rocks. Waves battered into the cove to smash mercilessly at *Otter*. Time and time again they had to start the engine to get way on her when the anchors dragged. It was cold during that long wet day and by nightfall it was colder still, with a banshee wind howling into the cove, piling icy surf up against the rocks and the stranded boat, and sloshing water mid-thigh deep about the men who worked on the outside of the hull. The men were holding the outer plywood in place as heavy bolts were pushed through the three layers of wood and tightened up, squeezing the pliant calking out at the edges. It was hard work, for the bolts were difficult to force through the swollen holes. Every now and then a great wave would shift the battered hull. Several times men went down full length beneath the waves.

Baldy kept a supply of hot coffee always on hand. There were hardly enough men to work in shifts, but no one complained. Mack's fighting spirit seemed to have sparked them all on. The boat was a valuable craft. She had been brought up clear from Seattle twenty-five hundred miles under her own power in company with four or five other boats, after having been ferried from Midway Island in the Pacific on the deck of a ship. After such a long trip, it was cruel indeed to think that she might rot on the lonely, fogbound coast of Atka without someone making an effort to save her.

The cold light of dawn revealed the fact that the hole was patched, and a bucketline was started to bail her out. Jim Brannon returned to the *Otter* to get the small, portable pump, which he brought back and set to work, but it would take time for the pump to clear the hull of water, so the bucket brigade kept on, passing the full buckets up to where they were dumped over the side to be refilled again, and again, and again.

It seemed to Bob that they were bailing a good part of the Bering Sea out of the PT boat, but by noon the hull was comparatively free of water and the rest of the planking seemed sound enough. Mack had towing lines attached to the stern cleats of the PT and taken out to *Otter*. Before they attempted to pull the boat free, they sat down to a meal for which Baldy had completely outdone himself.

"We'll have to turn *Otter* about," said Mack thoughtfully. " It won't be easy, but we can do it if we're careful."

"What about those seas smashing into the mouth of the cove, Skipper? " asked Thor. " With them to face and that hull dragging us back in the wash of the seas, we might pile up on the rocks."

"It's a chance we have to take." Mack stood up and filled his pipe, while his steady eyes flicked from one to the other of them. " Some of you men have had differences with me. Some of you failed in some of your duties. I'm forgetting all that now. You all did a good job getting *Otter* into this hole in the wall, and a first-rate job on the PT boat. But the real problem is ahead. To get out of this rock trap with that boat in tow. We'll have to make split-second decisions or we'll not only lose the tow boat but *Otter* as well. I don't have to tell you how dangerous it will be if *Otter* takes to the rocks."

It was very quiet in the small messroom. Every man there knew those treacherous and dangerous seas.

"Finish your coffee, lads," said Mack. " Be on deck in fifteen minutes. We've got work to do." He left the room and they heard his feet as he climbed the forward inside ladder to the interior of the pilothouse.

They all looked at one another. Smitty broke the silence. "Well," he said, "I'm Navy. We sure can use that boat. I'm game."

Mike Pucci nodded. "After the trip here and all the work we've done, there ain't no use in not trying at least to get her off."

Thor Andreason stood up and zipped his jacket shut. "We can't let Mack down," he said quietly. He left the room.

Jim Brannon emptied his cup. "Making that hull seaworthy is one thing; getting her off that beach and out'a this cove is another. I ain't sure at all, fellas."

"You aim to quit?" said Baldy angrily.

Jim looked at him mildly. "I ain't *sure*, I said, Baldy. I didn't say I wouldn't go along with the idea. Besides," he said with a quiet smile, "a fella can hardly quit out here, can he?"

Gary grinned. "That's what I was thinking."

Bob looked at Jesse. "We've heard from the Navy and the Merchant Marine," he said. "What about the Army, Jesse?"

"I'm whut they call a 'casual,' Robert," said Jesse quietly. "Besides, I think we kin do it. We got a good record. Ain't no use in spoilin' it now, is there?"

Bob shook his head and walked out onto the well deck. *Otter* was plunging and wallowing at her anchors. The seas had not subsided, nor would they from the looks of them.

Mack Dunbar leaned over the bridge railing. "No use waiting for this sea to subside," he said, almost as though he had read Bob's mind. "We'll do the best we can. If I think we'll lose *Otter*, we can cut the towing hawser."

"That'll be the day," said Gary under his breath as he

coiled a line and placed it on a belaying pin.

For an hour the decks of the *Otter* were filled with organized confusion. A spare kedge was taken astern in the powerboat and dropped to add to the holding power of the first one. The hawser from the PT boat was attached to the powerful winch on the forward deck. Surf was creaming about the stranded hull, spouting spray high along the stern and the sides.

Otter was put into slow reverse. The winch took up the strain and as the hawser tightened water spurted in thin jets from the compressed manila. The PT boat did not move. Again the winch whirred and the hawser tightened. A wave lifted up beneath the hull and the boat slid almost imperceptibly toward the deep water. If *Otter* could have been put into the full power of her reverse, the job could be done, but there was no chance of this, as the cove was too restricted, and beneath the surface of the disturbed water were many rocks waiting to rip into the hull of the boat.

A series of waves washed about the PT boat, lifting her up, and when they did, the winch clattered steadily, inching the hull down into the deeper water. Several times she struck rocks but the stout hull was not holed again. Then at last the hull floated free. Bob steered the powerboat alongside her, and Gary fastened a line about a cleat, so that they could hold her comparatively safe until *Otter* could be turned about. Gary dropped a small kedge from the PT boat over the stern and another over the bows while the hawser was slacked off from the *Otter*, then hauled aft and fastened to a strong bitt on the afterdeck of the boat. It wasn't the same as a towing winch, but it was the best they could do.

Slowly, taking advantage of wind and wave, *Otter* was

turned about like a toy boat in a small dishpan, scraping rocks several times, until she was headed into the seas that poured in wild confusion through the narrow mouth of the cove. Her bow anchors were dropped again to hold her there, and her engine kept her from putting too much strain on the anchor cables.

At a signal from Mack on the afterdeck of the *Otter*, Gary cut loose the kedges that held the PT boat to the bottom. Instantly she drifted back to take the bight out of the hawser, but she held steady, plunging and wallowing in the seas.

Bob steered back to the *Otter* and the powerboat was raised out of the water, but not swung inboard. They might have to leave *Otter* in a hurry. The lifeboat on the portside was also swung outboard, and every man aboard donned his lifejacket.

Mike Pucci went forward to the anchor winch. He pulled up the port anchor and looked back at Mack. For a moment Mack stood there, watching the seas, before he waved a hand. The winch clattered as *Otter* surged forward with three-quarter speed, taking up the slack in the anchor cable while Mike raced the winch to get the anchor free from the bottom, drawing it up until it hung in the hawsehole, ready to be dropped instantly if needed, and the odds were that both of those anchors would be needed.

Otter shuddered from stem to stern as the hawser took up with a snap, spraying water from the compressed strands. For a moment *Otter* seemed to lose way, then foot by foot she fought toward the narrow mouth of the cove, plunging deeply as she met the shock of the seas, dragging the dead weight of the wallowing PT boat behind her.

Every man except Jim Brannon was on deck. Jim was

nursing the throbbing diesel. Smitty stood beside the towing bitts with a sharp ax in his hands, waiting for the word to sever the towing hawser if it was necessary.

Thor Andreason was at the wheel, pale and taut-faced, gripping the spokes with both hands, flesh and mechanical, waiting for the sharp words of command from Mack Dunbar, who stood on the starboard wing bridge, glancing at the tow, then at the cove entrance, back and forth, big hands gripping the railing, unlighted pipe clenched in his blocky jaw.

Otter battered stubbornly into the thick seas. It didn't seem as though she was progressing at all. Again and again she drank deeply of the cold seas, flooding the decks, washing icy water about the legs of the men who stood there. They were oblivious of the chill, for life itself hung in the balance, and in a split second they might have to abandon their vessel for the hardly more hospitable shore.

The strain was terrible on the little vessel. She wallowed and rolled, bucked and swayed, as she struggled toward the open sea. Without the tow she could have made it easily. She was at full power now, squatting at the stern as the propeller fought for a hold in the water. Throbbing and trembling, shaking in every frame and plank, *Otter* edged closer and closer to the entrance.

Something thudded beneath the vessel. Bob felt his heart thud as well. Again came the ominous thudding noise. She was hitting bottom. The sound was like the knell of doom as the hull banged again and again, but suddenly she seemed free of the danger. She was even with the terrible rock arms of the cove, thrusting her blunt bows into the seas, driving into them with steady power. In five eternally long minutes she was free of the entrance. Far astern the PT boat seemed to hang back, fighting the seas as though reluctant to face the open water beyond the cove, but it wasn't her choice that day. *Otter* was the mistress, dragging her sister craft free from the icy and broken waters of the cove entrance, past the naked, black, and grinning rock formations until at last the PT boat was well free of that dangerous shore.

Otter was throttled down and she took the seas a little easier when Mack had the sails hoisted to steady her. She plunged on toward the northwest, making a wide sweep to clear the coast so as to round Cape Kigun.

Mike Pucci nestled a cup of coffee in his long and slender hands. " I never thought he'd make it," he said to Bob as Bob filled a cup for himself. " I'll swear he's a wizard. Him and this boat. I gotta admit it, kid. Why, he's *Navy*, he is! "

" I could have told you that all along," said Bob.

Otter seemed to rise up in the heaving seas as though to agree.

6

THE night was a maelstrom of rain, wind, waves, and spray as *Otter* bucked her way toward the dubious shelter of the lee afforded by hidden Tagalak Island somewhere off to starboard in the dark madness of the Aleutian storm.

Bob Dunbar fought his way forward on the upper deck of the pitching, rolling craft after checking the hawser and towing bitts. The hawser was sound, and there was no indication that the bitts had been started from their fastenings because of the sustained jerking and tugging of the PT boat lost in the howling madness astern of the towing vessel.

Bob timed himself, opened the door of the pilothouse as *Otter* rolled one way, stepped inside and slammed the door shut on its rollers as a shower of icy spray shot up the side of the boat and battered at the pilothouse side. "Who wouldn't sell a farm and go to sea?" he said as he wiped the salt spray from his numbed face.

"It'll make a man out of you," said Mike Pucci as he fought the wheel.

"Big deal," said Bob. "Where's Skipper?"

"Finally went below to get a little sleep. Beats me how he keeps on like he does."

"Speaking of men," said Bob with a sly grin.

Mike shot a smile at Bob, for he knew what Bob was referring to, and at that instant *Otter* seemed to lurch forward to batter herself into a headlong sea. She shuddered from stem to stern and keel to foretruck. Mike instantly rang for quarter speed to ease the vessel. He glanced at Bob.

"Tow line parted," said Bob. He timed himself again and slid the door open, jumped out on deck, and staggered aft past the lifeboat to peer down over the railing at the towing bitts on the small afterdeck. The line trailed into the wake of the *Otter*. He slid down the ladder and pulled in on the line. The hawser had parted cleanly twenty feet from the stern of the *Otter*. Somewhere astern of them was the drifting PT boat.

Thor Andreason thrust his head out of a stern door. "Parted?" he asked. "I could feel it in the engine room."

Bob nodded, holding up the frayed end of the hawser. It was nothing more than he had expected. Maybe now they could run ahead of the battering seas and ease the hard-pressed *Otter*. "Tell the skipper," he said.

Mack Dunbar was up in the pilothouse minutes after Thor had warned him about the parting of the hawser. The *Otter* turned into the teeth of the storm to hunt for the lost tow, and as she did so, it seemed impossible that she could stand such seas for very long. Bob had never seen anything like it in his time on the Bering and the North Pacific, even in the notorious Gulf of Alaska.

Thor Andreason came into the pilothouse. "Jim says we can't stand too much of this, Skipper."

Mack Dunbar held the wheel in his big hands, half-closed eyes squinting through the wet glass of the window in front of him. "We won't have to," he said out of the side of his mouth. "There she is."

The PT boat was plunging up and down, with the

hawser trailing off into the sea. *Otter* moved closer to her until the PT boat was a hundred yards away.

"You'll never keep her on the end of that hawser unless you have some steerageway on her," said Thor quietly. "If we can get that one engine started, it might do the trick."

"I'll risk no one aboard that craft," said Mack.

"You're risking us all by towing her this way," said Thor quietly.

Mack did not answer. Thor was right.

"We either get some steerageway on her, Skipper, or we'll lose her again, if we don't lose *Otter* as well," said Thor.

"I hate to give up," said Mack.

"We all do," said Thor. "It's our fight as well as yours."

Otter shuddered in the slamming seas.

"Someone has to stay aboard her," said Mack at last.

"When I suggested the idea," said Thor, "I intended that I would do the job."

"You can't do it alone," said Mack.

Bob knew what his uncle was thinking. He remembered too well how Thor had failed at the helm when the Japanese submarine had opened fire on *Otter*. *Otter* had nearly been lost that time. Supposing he failed again aboard the PT boat?

"I know engines," said Thor. "I can keep that engine going if anyone can."

"You'll need a man at the helm, Thor."

Otter wallowed and plunged, taking water full over her bows as she edged closer and closer to the PT boat.

"I can ask for a volunteer, Skipper," said the young man.

Bob took his courage in his hands. He wanted that PT boat saved as much as his uncle did. The whole crew wanted to save that boat. In a sense, the PT boat was far

70

more valuable to the Government, and the campaign in the Aleutians, than *Otter* could possibly be worth. " I'll go," he said.

" No," said Mack.

" I have the right to volunteer," stated Bob.

" Not as my nephew," snapped Mack. " Supposing you were lost? How could I ever face your parents? "

" Thor lost his brother," said Bob. " How would his parents feel if he was lost as well? "

" That's no argument! "

" I'm a signed member of this crew," said Bob. " I have the right to volunteer. Besides, I can handle a helm as good as any man aboard this bucket, and you know it, Skipper."

Thor eyed Mack. " I served aboard PT boats before I was assigned to the *Nevada*," he said. " I can brief Bob about their little tricks. I can't do the job alone, Skipper."

Mack did not look at Bob. " All right," he grated.

It took timing to bring *Otter* alongside the pitching PT boat, but Thor made the leap easily, followed by Bob, who landed lightly on the resilient sponge-rubber deck. Bob pulled the parted hawser up over the side and passed it to the *Otter*, where it was made fast to the towing bitts. Lines held the PT boat alongside *Otter* while Jim Brannon clambered aboard to give Thor a hand in starting the one engine. If Jim couldn't start it, no one could.

Bob climbed to the narrow, open bridge and eyed the controls. He knew he could handle the boat all right. It was the weather that would bother him, but there was no choice. He was bundled in a parka that was water-repellent and the bridge would shield him to some extent.

It took an hour for the engine to start kicking over, and it ran erratically, but enough to give the boat steerageway to take some of the terrible strain from the hawser. Once the engine started and ticked over, Jim returned to his engine room on *Otter*, while the PT boat was allowed to drift free. Bob felt the PT boat take up the slack in the hawser. He kept enough way on her to ease the strain and keep the boat from yawing too wildly. It was all he could do to keep his footing as the boat pitched and plunged, but he knew she was towing better. Ahead of him, dimly seen through the flying water and darkness, was a light on the stern of *Otter*. That, and the dripping hawser, were seemingly the only links that held him to the world of life and warmth. Time and time again he thought of Thor Andreason, down in the pitching engine room, tending the balky engine, fighting a battle of nerves to keep from panicking, for if the great wooden patch on the bow of the boat broke loose, the boat would go to the bottom like a stone, and there'd be no hope for Thor Andreason.

Hour after hour the two boats slogged through the hell of that stormy night. When Bob had given up hope that light would ever appear again, he suddenly realized it was breaking daylight through the storm rack flying overhead. The stern of the *Otter* came into view, and soon he could make her out quite clearly. Someone was standing beside the towing bitts, muffled in a parka, and he knew well enough who it was. It must be his uncle.

Bob estimated they were somewhere off Omak Island by now. That would place their position twenty-five to thirty miles from the harbor at Adak. The storm seemed to be blowing itself out. He looked to windward and felt cold seep into his inner soul. The storm was abating, but Old Man Weather wasn't through yet with his Pandora's box of tricks. He was replacing the howling wind with thick fog that was moving across the heaving seas like some poisonous gas. In a matter of minutes the *Otter* had van-

72

ished from sight and the only connection with her was the dripping hawser that seemed to vanish into the fog as though it was extending into a fourth dimension, still there, but unseen.

Thor came wearily up on deck and peered at Bob. " How does it go? " he asked.

" Cold, and wet," said Bob. " At least you were warm down there."

Thor nodded. " Warm, but a little sick. The fumes are thick. The engine seems to be running as well as can be expected. How long before we make Adak? "

" In this fog? Who knows? Six to eight hours more or less."

Thor shook his head. " So near and yet so far."

The motor throbbed and missed, throbbed and missed. Thor darted below. In minutes it began to run more evenly.

It must be close to noon, thought Bob, hours after the fog had settled in over the islands. They must be somewhere off the end of Omak Island, feeling their way through the swirling and icy breath of the fog, like blind men. Bob passed a hand across his eyes. Something snapped up forward. He heard a faint splashing sound and the motion of the boat changed. He leaned forward to look across the top of the bridge toward the forward deck and what he saw made him sick clean through. The hawser had vanished, taking the cleats and towing bitts along with it. The PT boat was moving through the fog at a snail's pace under her own power.

He tried to peer through the fog, but it was no use. The swirling opaqueness played strange tricks with his eyes and mind. Fifteen minutes passed and there was no sight or sound of *Otter* — nothing but the swirling fog shrouding the PT boat like a winding sheet of the dead. Fear came through the fog on noiseless wings and settled on the deck of the PT boat.

Thor appeared on the deck. " What's wrong? " he asked.

" Tow line pulled cleats and bitts from the deck, Thor," said Bob. " I thought maybe *Otter* would be back for us by now."

" In this soup? "

Bob passed a hand across his eyes. " Maybe it was wishful thinking."

" Where are we? "

" Somewhere off Omak."

Thor rubbed his jaws. " From what I recall of the chart, there are two or three other islands close to Omak."

" West of it are Little Tanaga and Kagalaska. North of it are some smaller islands. I don't know their names."

" Great! First thing we know we'll hit one of them and we won't have to worry about its name."

" At this speed? "

Thor peered into the fog. " We could hit bottom, kid," he said quietly. " Rocks as sharp as razors could rip this plywood hull to shreds. If we miss the underwater rocks and are driven ashore, she won't take much of a pounding."

" We haven't hit yet," said Bob.

Thor looked quickly at him. " There speaks the brave heart," he said. " I wish *I* felt so optimistic. Do we have a compass? "

" No. They stripped most everything of value off her when they abandoned her."

" Any charts? "

" A wet one in that locker there. Won't do much good to have a chart if we don't know where we are."

" What do we do now? "

74

Bob eased the helm a little. "Keep moving, I guess. Either *Otter* will find us, or we can drift around until the fog lifts and try to get some bearings."

"That might take days, kid."

Bob shrugged. "What else do we have to do?"

"No water and no food aboard. I never thought of it."

Bob stared into the fog. Somewhere, within yards of them, there might be the jagged rocks Thor had mentioned. their only hope was to hear the surf against the rocks before they came too close to the rocks — too close to get out to sea again.

Thor went below to check the engine, leaving Bob alone to face the fog and the heaving seas, and he had never felt so alone in his entire life.

He wasn't too worried about going ashore, if they weren't piled up on the rocks, for there would be fresh water on any island they might land on. That was one blessing of the constant rains in the Aleutians, and they could somehow contrive to catch fish to stay alive until they were found. It was the thought of losing the PT boat after all the hardships and dangers they had gone through to save her.

Maybe they'd idle through one of the channels between the islands and find themselves off Adak by the time the fog lifted. The cold thought came through his mind that Japanese submarines came boldly close in to Adak at times. They had been seen and one of them had been reported sunk by aerial bombardment, for the planes had seen a telltale oil slick on the surface, which didn't mean absolute proof that the sub had been sunk. Submariners were a wily bunch, and they had been known to release oil from a submerged boat to give the impression it had been permanently sunk by bombs or depth charges. If one of them found the PT boat, there'd be no trace left of her, or her temporary crew of two. The boat had hardly enough speed to outrun even a sub on the surface, although they could do as much as fifty knots under full power in ordinary circumstances.

The seas were dying down, but the fog was getting thicker. Bob felt as though they had wandered clear off the face of the earth and were in a world of fog and water that would stretch endlessly into eternity. There was little sound other than the rather unsteady throbbing of the engine, the lapping of the water against the sides of the hull, and the moaning of the wind. The fog itself had no voice, which made it all the more eerie and unreal.

Thor came up on deck and held out a handful of hard crackers to Bob. " Found these in a locker," he said. "Emergency rations. Better than nothing. I'll look around and see if I can find rainwater collected in something." He was back in ten minutes with a cup full of rainwater. " Best I could do," he said. " We can split it."

There was absolutely nothing they could do to better their condition — nothing but move slowly through the clinging fog and hope for the best.

" Listen! " said Thor suddenly.

The sound of heavy surf came to them from port. A moment later they heard it from the starboard side as well.

" Maybe we've drifted into a cove or harbor," said Thor.

Bob peered into the fog. Any minute now he expected the boat to take bottom, maybe to founder, and a man would never know which way to swim in the few minutes he would have to survive in those frigid waters.

The pounding of the surf grew louder, drowning out the sound of the engine. Louder and louder it became, until Bob was sure it was only a matter of minutes before they would see the waves crashing over harsh black rock. Then slowly the sound seemed to retreat, and twenty minutes later he could see that the fog was thinning, although there was still too much of it to see where they were.

Thor was below, nursing the engine, when Bob saw the first sign of land, far to starboard, and then minutes later he saw land far to port. Astern was the channel they had come through, hardly a quarter of a mile wide, edged by rocky shores upon which the seas crashed steadily, sending up great showers of spray.

Ahead of them was more open sea. Bob thought they might have drifted between either Omak and Little Tanaga, or perhaps Little Tanaga and Kagalaska, although in the mist it was hard to determine whether those were the islands he thought they were. If they were, then they were not too far from Kulik Bay on Adak, and if they could get a landfall, they could recognize before the fog socked in again, and if Thor could keep the balky engine going, they might make it to the safety of Adak.

The fog was clearing as the wind arose, and Bob thought he saw humped mountains rising out of the sea ahead of them, in the general direction of Adak. There would be patrol craft about, and perhaps a friendly plane might spot them.

Then he heard the noise. The humming of a plane's engines above the overcast. He looked up in the general direction of the noise and thought he saw something moving through the overcast. A moment later a PBY moved through the sky in a somewhat clearer area. The wind had thinned away some of the fog between the boat and the island ahead of it and Bob was sure it was Adak. It would only be a matter of minutes before the plane would see them. Perhaps it was conducting a search for them.

The engine coughed and spat, coughed and spat again, then throbbed erratically for a time, driving the boat closer and closer to Adak. Bob had hard work to keep it heading for the island. With one propeller turning, the boat had a tendency to move constantly to port, and if left to her own helm, she would describe wide circles. He was so busy fighting the helm he did not see the PBY until it was close by, flashing a signal light from one of the side blisters. It swept past and vanished into the overcast.

Bob leaned over and checked the signal lamp. It would not light up. Then he realized he did not know the recognition signal. " Thor! " he yelled.

Thor popped out on deck. " Yes? "

" Do you know the recognition signal? "

" I think so."

" See if you can get this lamp lighted."

The PBY was coming back, lower this time, winging slowly past as the signal lamp in the blister flicked on and off, almost impatiently.

" It's no use," said Thor. " I can't get this thing lighted."

They stared up at the PBY as it swung in a wide arc and vanished into the overcast. The PT boat wallowed slowly toward the island. There wasn't another boat of any kind in sight, Navy or Merchant Marine, although the fog in the distance might conceal many things.

Thor stared at the lowering sky. The humming sound came again and this time the PBY was flying lower and lower, slanting down toward the boat. " She's going to land and take us off maybe," said Thor.

Closer and closer the ungainly-looking amphibian came and her signal lamp flicked rapidly. As she passed and received no signal from the PT boat, something else flashed from the blister, and the horrified crew of the boat saw tracers flicking through the air toward them, some of them striking the sea and bouncing off.

" She's shooting at us! " yelled Thor. He stared wildly about, and Bob remembered his panic the time the Japanese submarine had fired at *Otter*.

The PBY climbed, banked, and returned, this time firing from the other blister as she passed to port of the slowly moving boat. A tracer skipped across the water and then something tore into the deck twenty feet behind the bridge. Bob hit the deck. The engine spluttered and died.

Back again came the PBY and something dropped from beneath her. Two dark objects slanted toward the boat. They struck close alongside and detonated. The PT boat seemed to rear up out of the water as the bombs exploded. Wood shattered. Machine guns flashed inside the low overcast and tracers flicked down. Bullets tore into the broken hull. The boat began to settle a little in the water.

Bob crawled out on the deck, trying to keep something between him and those deadly fifty caliber slugs. Thor was lying facedown on the deck, his body shaking like an aspen leaf. It was then that Bob heard the roaring of more engines and a peculiar whining sound. He peered around the front of the bullet-pocked bridge. Three planes were diving at the boat. There was no mistaking the type. Twin-engined and twin-boomed, spitting flames from their blunt noses. The feared P-38 Lightnings had evidently been summoned by the PBY to aid her in her battle.

A storm of slugs smashed into the sinking craft. Bob stared wildly about. In the distance he saw a familiar sight. *Otter* was surging toward them with a bone in her teeth. Her signal lamp was flickering insistently.

The P-38's seemed to hang in the sky and then down they came again. Machine-gun fire flickered, and tracers reached out hungrily for the dying boat.

"Over the side!" screamed Bob at Thor.

The man did not move. Bob had no choice. He man-handled Thor over the side, heard him splash as he hit the icy water. Bob dropped in beside him, sinking deeply, but bobbing to the surface as his life jacket carried him up. The shock of the water drove the breath from his body and his head hit the side of the PT boat. She was very low in the water.

Once more the rain of slugs smashed into the PT boat and the three Lightnings soared upward into the overcast. The deck of the boat was level with the water. She rolled heavily and with a gurgling rush she went below, leaving a litter of trash and bits of broken wood on the water in the froth of her sinking. The humming of the plane engines died away in the overcast.

The last thing Bob remembered before he passed out in the icy waters was seeing *Otter* plowing at full speed toward the two of them.

7

IN EARLY December, *Otter* swung at two anchors, deep-seated in the bottom of the harbor, plunging and fighting to free herself from the hooks as the howling wind lashed at Adak, roaring down from the snow-clad mountains, screaming in mad fury across the surface of the harbor, piling barges, small craft, and PBY's up on the foaming black sand beaches. The huge new wooden pier sagged as a massive transport, a great wind catcher, pressed hard against it. The wind had not stopped for twenty-four hours and showed no sign of decreasing. Sometimes it was only wind and at other times it drove icy rain or stinging snow horizontally across the harbor.

Mack Dunbar was down in the small forward hold of the pitching vessel, peering here and there, flicking his flashlight to cover every inch of planking and ribbing. Water sloshed back and forth at his feet and the steady throbbing of the pumps had not stopped for twenty-four hours, ever since the fierce wind had roared down on the Aleutians, and particularly on the Andreanof group of islands.

Bob held on to a stanchion as *Otter* rolled deeply. The small vessel had been leaking somewhat from the time she had struck bottom the day they had hauled the doomed PT out of the cove on Atka Island. He remembered quite well how she had thudded against the harsh bottom of the cove. Something had happened to her stout sheathed planking and frames up forward. The long tow after that, dragging the reluctant PT boat after her until the hawser had parted, hadn't done *Otter* any good either.

Mack looked back at Bob. " It's no use, kid," he said quietly. " We can't calk her from the inside, and there's no way we can get her out of the water here at Adak to work on her from the outside. She's done her best; worked her heart out."

" The pumps are keeping the water out," said Bob.

Mack nodded. " Heavy seas will work on the hull until the leak gets worse, and if it does, she'll leak like a basket. I'm afraid I'll have to get permission to take her back to Dutch, or Kodiak, maybe even to the mainland. It's either that, or lose her. No use in making heroes out of ourselves. They need *Otter* badly, but in this condition they won't have her very long."

They climbed up the ladder into the narrow tween-decks and walked aft, grabbing stanchions every so often as the vessel heaved and pitched. " Well," said Bob, " they won't let us leave in this kind of weather. In fact, no vessels are coming in or going out."

They entered the lower deck of the after superstructure. Jim Brannon stuck his head out of the little engine room. " Skipper," he said quietly, " how much longer will we have to stay out here in the islands? "

Mack shrugged. " Just until I get permission to take her back for hull repairs."

" Good. We need some work done on this engine. She's not too bad, but if we keep running her this way, I won't guarantee results."

Mack nodded. " It doesn't surprise me, Jim."

Bob followed his uncle into the messroom for coffee.

One thing after another was plaguing the little ship. She had done hard and arduous service ever since the strike at Dutch Harbor in June, when she had been badly damaged. Bigger ships of steel were being pounded to pieces in Aleutian service. It was a wonder that *Otter* was afloat at all.

November had blown in with a vicious storm, howling all the way across the Bering Sea from Siberia. Eighty-knot winds had blasted the island, sweeping a foot of water across the airfield. In five months' time the Air Corps and Navy had lost over eighty planes, many of them from weather damage, some of which had been destroyed on the ground. Time and time again the fliers had been forced to hole up in their quonset huts and tents, while ships beat to the dubious shelter of wind-lashed harbors. There had been no question of fighting a war then, but rather one of fighting the weather, and the only satisfaction was that the Japanese on Kiska and Attu were doing the same thing.

Bob had an idea what was bothering his uncle. Rumor was rife that the powers that be were planning to advance farther along the chain to occupy another island, or islands. Some said it would be Tanaga, which would hardly be of much advantage, for it was only about forty-five or fifty miles from Adak. Others held out for Amchitka, which had a good harbor, as Aleutian harbors go, and possibilities of a good building site for an airstrip. It was one hundred and forty miles west of Adak and only sixty miles east of Kiska, the Japanese-occupied island, which would be the next logical objective once the offensive began in the spring. Rumor also had it that the Army opposed the move to Amchitka, while the Navy wanted it. If the move was made to Amchitka, coming closer to grips with the enemy, Mack Dunbar wanted to be in on it, and he seemed to know it would be only a matter of months, or perhaps even weeks.

"Maybe we can get back in time," said Bob quietly.

His uncle looked up quickly from his coffee cup. "You have your mother's knack of seeming to read minds, kid."

"I've been aboard *Otter* long enough to be able to figure some things out," said Bob. He refilled his cup. "They won't let you take *Otter* out there in the condition she's in. We'll have to go back and trust to luck we can return in time."

Mack nodded. "Might get a chance to see your mother," he said. "If you can cadge a lift from Dutch or Kodiak."

Bob grinned and shook his head. "No you don't," he said quickly. "I'm staying with *Otter* even in dry dock. No chance of you getting me out of the way, when you head back out here again."

"You've had two close ones now, kid. The third time may be the out."

"It might also be the charm."

"You've got your mother's sense and your father's stubbornness."

"I seem to know someone else who's a little stubborn."

Mack drained his cup. "That's enough of that," he growled. "Get about your duties."

Bob shrugged into his parka and went up on deck. The skies were a muddy gray and the mountains were clothed in icy white snow, while the harbor surface was a mass of heaving water broken into flying spray and foam. *Otter* was plunging deeply, dragging at her hooks. The pumps were still operating, the dirty water from the bilges was running across the dirtier deck and flowing from the scuppers. Now and then the clean seawater would sweep the

84

decks fore and aft, but it seemed as though nothing could really clean them except a scraping and holystoning. Bob eyed the rigging. Some of the shrouds needed replacing. The canvas sail covers were patched and stained. Rust showed scabrously here and there. Dents and scratches marked the once-smooth decks. *Otter* was showing more and more signs of her war service.

Between snow squalls he could see the other gray-painted ships wallowing and plunging at their anchors. Dirty snow covered the tents, quonsets, and supply dumps. Smoke from funnels and chimneys lay flat as it streamed in the howling wind. It was a dreary and lonesome sight, despite the fact that thousands of men were within the area of a few miles, though out of sight. The planes were in their revetments, their engines shrouded in canvas, unable to take to the air in such weather. The war in the Aleutians, such as it was, was definitely at a stalemate, and yet, beneath all the dreariness and the intense loneliness there was a feeling of life, a feeling that it would not be long before the westward movement began once again. Bob wanted to be in on it.

Gary came up on deck and handed Bob a huge piece of gingerbread. "I told Baldy he could use this for an extra anchor if we started to drag. I don't think he liked it. Anyway, I made sure I said it *after* he gave me two pieces."

"One of these days," warned Bob.

"He loves me," said Gary. "Like a father loves a prodigal son. You hear the news?"

"What news?"

"As soon as the storm blows over we have to take a load of supplies and some replacements to an outpost near Cape Yakok. I hear it gets pretty rough out there."

"That's all we need," said Bob. "Leaky hull, faulty engine, the whole bit. Maybe they mean to smash us up entirely so they don't have to bother about sending us back for repairs. I wouldn't put it past them."

"Maybe you don't know it, buddy," said Gary, "but there happens to be a war on."

Bob finished his gingerbread. "We'd better get busy," he said.

The supply barge was towed out to them later that day, and despite the heaving and pitching of the barge and *Otter*, the supplies and replacements and a handful of infantrymen were safely transferred aboard *Otter*. She was deeper in the water with the weight of the supplies and rode easier, but the water was leaking in faster. The thudding of the pumps never stopped.

By nightfall, such as it was, the storm had abated somewhat, and by the following dawn, *Otter* put to sea and headed for distant Cape Yakok, through a misty fog that hung high above the water, draping down here and there like a bridal veil, and when the *Otter* plowed through the veils it was like soft, icy fingers touching one's face. *Otter* kept well offshore, being steered by compass. Bob was at the helm, and the feeling was strong within him that this would be the last trip for *Otter* until she was through being refitted back at Dutch or Kodiak. He was sorry in one way and yet happy in another. He wanted to see his mother and his younger brother, Sandy, and sister, Lynn, back at Anchorage if he had the time. On the other hand, he did not want to miss the westward push that was sure to come in the near future. They had missed the Adak landing and he didn't want to miss the next one, wherever it might be — Tanaga, Amchitka, or Kiska itself, or perhaps even distant Attu. The very name of Attu gave him a little chill as he shifted the helm to avoid a log, idly wondering as he did so where the log had come from, perhaps Japan itself. It was said that the Japanese had tough Marines and veteran infantrymen entrenched on Attu, well-armed, and backed by hidden artillery, with surface and underwater craft patrolling offshore. The Japanese were tough and tenacious. It wouldn't be easy to pry them loose from their holds on Kiska and Attu.

He watched the bilge water sloshing back and forth on the well deck, about the tarpaulined supplies lashed there. The pumps were still holding their own. If they hit another storm, or sudden howling williwaw sweeping out of a mountain gorge to hit the sea about *Otter*, she might not survive. Another chilling thought struck Bob. Maybe his uncle had been right. Bob had had two narrow escapes in his months in the Aleutians — his wounding in the second air raid at Dutch, and his experiences on the PT boat. Since that day, Thor Andreason had hardly said a word to Bob, or anyone else aboard the *Otter*, for that matter. Twice he had broken under fire, and twice Mack Dunbar had refused to ask him to leave the *Otter*. " The third time is out," said Bob aloud.

" What do you mean, kid? " said Mack Dunbar from behind Bob.

Bob jumped. " I didn't know you were in the pilothouse, Skipper," he said with a red face.

" Just came in. What did you mean? "

" Nothing, sir."

Mack walked to the front of the pilothouse, checked the compass bearing. He began to fill his pipe. " I know you did mean something. What is it, Bob? "

" Thor Andreason, Skipper."

Mack lighted his pipe. " You have to have faith in a man," he said between puffs.

87

" That much? "

Mack nodded. " That much and more, kid. Much more. Again and again, and again — "

" Even if it endangers the ship and the crew? " said Bob quietly.

" A man has to have time to find himself, kid. Someday the experience will come to you. It won't be a pleasant one."

" Has it happened to you? "

Mack nodded. He blew out a smoke ring. " More times than I care to admit," he said.

Mack Dunbar said nothing more while Bob was doing his trick at the wheel. Later on that day as *Otter* slogged through the heaving seas toward Cape Yakok, Bob had plenty of time to think about his uncle's words. Maybe by the time they had *Otter* refitted and repaired Thor Andreason would be able to orient himself. Maybe he'd take the unspoken hints of the rest of the crew and leave *Otter* when she was back at Dutch or Kodiak. The Bering is a tough opponent of men and ships. There is no place for a weakling, or an unfit ship in those waters.

They eased in toward Cape Yakok in the early dusk, urged on by a deceptively smooth ground swell. There was powerful liquid strength beneath the greasy-looking swells. The wind was fitful, veering back and forth, at times off the starboard beam or quarter, then veering full astern, making steering difficult.

Every man jack was on duty as *Otter* crept in toward the lowering black headland, capped with streaked snow. The channel into the narrow cove passed close beneath the rough-looking cliffside, towering high above the small vessel, almost seeming to lean dangerously over the *Otter* as though threatening her.

It was ticklish business. Gary Lunt was at the wheel, watching Mack Dunbar, who clung to the starboard shrouds not ten feet from the cliff face, scanning the heaving waters, guiding Gary by hand signals. Inch by inch, or so it seemed, *Otter* felt her way into the cove. She had been there several times before, and it never seemed to get easier, rather, more difficult.

At the far end of the cove on the rocky beach stood a handful of men muffled in hooded parkas, rifles slung over their shoulders, watching the *Otter* creep into the cove. Higher up the slopes behind them could be seen the tips of pyramidal tents, with stovepipes sticking above them emitting thin tendrils of bluish smoke. Higher still was the radio aerial, well guyed and braced against the wild winds. To one side was the lip of a sandbagged machine gun emplacement, from which protruded the snout of a canvas-covered machine gun, covering the cove entrance. It was a forlorn and lonely place, as most of the outposts were in those islands.

Otter reached her mooring place, and her anchor plunged to the bottom. Minutes later the powerboat was surging toward the beach, heavily laden with men and supplies. On the return trip she brought back the two men who were to return with *Otter*. It took three hours to land all the supplies and mail. A heavy fog was drifting across the open sea, stealing in toward the land. It would be a matter of minutes before *Otter* would have to poke her way out of the cove.

The anchor was dripping at the starboard hawsehole when a man came running down to the beach from the radio station on the bluff overlooking the cove, waving a sheet of paper. The powerboat was already being raised from the water. Mack Dunbar saw the man on the beach and the stealthy approach of the fog. "What is it?" he yelled.

"Message from headquarters, sir!"

Mack shouted: "Lower the boat! Get ashore and get that message! Waste no time! We've got to beat that fog before it comes into the cove or we'll be here for hours! Jump and make it so!"

The boat splashed into the water. Bob started the motor and steered for shore, nuzzling the bows into the black sand. The radioman handed the paper to Smitty, who was in the bows. Bob reversed the motor, cleared the beach, put the motor into forward, and sped back toward *Otter*, the powerboat plunging deeply as she met the heavy swells working into the cove and dashing from the cliffside. The falls were quickly hooked on as the boat came alongside *Otter*. Bob cut the motor. The falls whirred as the heavy boat was raised. Bob stepped over the side and helped settle the boat into its chocks and make it fast.

As swiftly as the crew worked they could not beat the entering of the fog into the cove. In the swirling mistiness the vessel was turned, and at dead slow speed she worked her way toward the mouth of the cove, Mack Dunbar at the port shrouds, close to the cliff face, the radio message sticking out of the side pocket of his pea coat. *Otter* surged dangerously close to the rugged cliff face as she fought the incoming waves, poking her blunt nose into the bewildering vagueness of the fog.

Mack Dunbar signaled and Gary eased away from the cliff. Another signal and he veered in close again — so close that Mack could have put out a foot and touched the naked black rock. It was touch and go now, a matter of minutes while the *Otter*'s weathered side passed inches away from the cruel rock. A minute to go and then the engine missed, took up a steady beating, missed again and again, losing power. A great wave flowed into the cove, raising the surface of the water, and as it passed *Otter*, it lifted her easily and powerfully upward and slammed her against the cliff face. Mack Dunbar swung inboard at the very moment *Otter* struck with stunning force. "Full speed ahead" he roared.

The motor skipped and missed, then took up a full-throated roaring, but it was a little too late, for once more *Otter* took her medicine, the price of Aleutian service. Something cracked dully as she broke free from the face of the cliff and surged toward the fog-wreathed open sea. Mack hung over the side, passing a hand along the timbers of his vessel. He stood up and walked toward the bridge with a set look on his face. *Otter* was taking too much of a beating. He climbed slowly to the bridge and entered the pilothouse. He looked back at the cliff face, now hardly to be seen in the gray, shifting mist.

Bob was at the wheel when his uncle opened the spray-wet radio message scrawled in pencil on a form. He stared at it. His lips parted. He read it again and shook his head. He walked to the chart table and pulled out a chart which he studied intently. He turned and came back to Bob, instructing him as to compass course. Bob looked at him quickly. "Begging your pardon, Skipper," he said, "isn't that the wrong way to go?"

"Not according to the message."

"What did it say, sir?"

Mack Dunbar slowly filled his pipe and then lighted it. "We're to go to Ulak Island," he said quietly, "beyond Tanaga Pass, and pick up a party of Alaskan Scouts who have been investigating a rumor that Japs were seen on the island. We're to bring them back to Dutch Harbor with us

91

rather than return to Adak. When we reach Dutch we can get our repairs." He smashed a fist into his other palm. " Couldn't they have sent someone else? We're in no condition to face a williwaw in these waters, kid."

" How far is it, Skipper? "

" About ninety miles of fairly open water. We'll pass south of Kanaga and Tanaga Islands, and hope to miss Ilak Island, such as it is, in the fog. I hope the fog lifts before we reach Ulak. Those are dangerous waters even for the Aleutians. Why couldn't they have sent someone else? "

Bob eased the helm a little. " It's getting to be a tough war out here, Skipper."

Mack shot a glance at his nephew's impassive face. " Seems to me I said those very words, kid."

" You did, sir."

Mack smiled. " Don't complain and don't explain, eh? "

Bob grinned. " You're getting to be *Navy*, Skipper."

Otter hunched down and took a deep one over her bows. The pumps were hard at work, and frequently the engine skipped a beat. Instead of heading east for shelter and repairs, *Otter* was forging west along the dangerous chain of islands, in a thick fog, on a rough sea, to do her duty. Ships and men were expendable in those seas — *the cold seas beyond.*

8

ULAK ISLAND was off the starboard beam, dimly visible through the drifting fog, seemingly an enchanted island, seen only through the magical incantations of some evil shaman of the Aleutians. There wasn't a sign of life to be seen through the shifting veils of fog. The heavy breakers creamed on the black sand and sprayed high above the edged rocks. The gray-green valleys between the rounded hills were devoid of life.

Otter moved slowly along the east coast of the small island, with three binoculars being used by the best eyes in the crew, studying the terrain foot by foot, while others of the crew peered through the uneasy wreaths of fog trying to spot a signal or a movement on the empty-looking island.

Bob Dunbar swayed back and forth in the crow's nest, eyes glued to the powerful binoculars, moving his head slowly as he scanned the island. Surely they would have been spotted by now, but there were no signals, nothing to indicate that the Alaskan Scouts, supposedly alerted by radio, would be waiting somewhere along those lonely beaches for *Otter*.

Bob knew some of the members of the Alaskan Scouts very well. They were rugged men, more used to outdoor life than living in houses and in towns. Fishermen, hunters, and trappers. They knew the remote places of Alaska and the Aleutians as few other men did. Time after time they had been dropped off at remote islands by plane, submarine, or surface craft to vanish into the fog, with camouflaged equipment, rifles painted gray, green, and brown, faces daubed like Indian warriors so that they would blend unseen with their surroundings.

Mack Dunbar paced the starboard wing of the little bridge. "We'll have to round the south point and work up the western side of the island," he said.

They all knew what that meant. The offshore set was against the western side of the island, and if *Otter*'s engine failed, they'd have to rely on the worn sails to get them out to safer waters. That wouldn't be easy, for they'd have to beat against the freshening wind.

The uneasy thought came to Bob that maybe the Scouts *had* found the Japanese on Ulak, or rather the Japanese had found *them* first. It would have been a murderous little fight in the fog and cold, no quarter given or asked for in the manner of guerrilla warfare. Maybe even now enemy eyes were watching *Otter* as she wallowed slowly along the coast. Maybe they had a gun big enough to sink her, or at least damage her enough to put her out of action. Perhaps even a submarine was lurking in one of the coves, tracking *Otter* with her gunsights, or was lying beneath the heaving swells of the sea, following *Otter* with the one deadly eye of the periscope. *Otter* was far west of Adak, the strongest American outpost in the Aleutians. Beyond Adak were nothing but tiny isolated outposts — submarine, surface, and air patrols of both American and Japanese forces. It was no place for *Otter*.

Slowly, ever so slowly, they rounded the southern tip of Ulak and worked up the western coast against the strong offshore set, still studying the silent, empty-looking hills and valleys of the island.

Bob knew what his uncle was thinking. It wasn't up to him to have to land and hunt for the Scouts. They should have been ready to receive *Otter* and come aboard her. Mack could easily give orders to return east to safety, but it wasn't like him. He edged *Otter* in closer and closer until she was pitching and wallowing not five hundred yards from the bleak shore, with a tiny islet off the port bow.

" Bob! " called out Mack Dunbar. " Come down! I can use you here! "

Bob scuttled down the ratlines and handed the glasses to his relief. Mack Dunbar was leaning on the railing of the wing bridge looking at the shore. " Kid," he said quietly, " I'm going to send a boat ashore with a few men in it to hunt for those boys. You don't have to go if you don't want to, but you can handle the powerboat in surf better than any man aboard."

" Except you, Skipper," said Bob.

Mack nodded. " I can't leave *Otter*," he said. " Much as I'd like to do the job, I can't leave my responsibility here. Take Gary along if you like."

" I'll go, sir," said a quiet voice.

Down on the well deck, one of the infantrymen from Cape Yakok was looking up at them. He was a rugged-looking, broad-shouldered man of about twenty-five, with a short reddish beard, definitely not regulation.

" I'm Corporal Chuck MacIver," said the man. " Of the Alaskan Scouts. I was assigned to Cape Yakok outpost with Bennie Dutton. He's a half-breed, mother was an Aleut from up Sanak way, and his father knew these islands like a native Aleut. We'd like to volunteer to go along."

Mack smiled. " I thought you boys were just infantry

guards for Cape Yakok outpost."

Chuck grinned as he tugged at his beard. " With this? " He picked up his rifle. It was a Springfield bolt action, painted in soft mottled colors of gray, green, and brown. "We're the only outfit out here that could get away with messing up a perfectly good .30/06 rifle like this."

A squat-looking man came up beside Chuck MacIver. He was short-legged for his height, and his face was broad and flat. There wasn't any doubt it was Bennie Dutton, the half-breed who was Chuck MacIver's partner.

Mack nodded his head. "All right, boys. Let's get the powerboat into the water."

In a matter of minutes the powerboat had been lowered into the water. Chuck and Bennie dropped into it, followed by Gary Lunt, who unhooked the falls and kept the boat alongside with the boathook. Mack Dunbar silently handed Bob a pair of issue .45 caliber Colts, complete with belts, holsters, and cartridge pouches. " I don't think you'll need these," he said, " but I've shown you and Gary how to use them. You never know what you'll run into in these islands. Watch yourself, kid. There's a war on out here."

Later, as Bob steered for the cove Mack had indicated to him, he looked back at *Otter*, now making her way farther from the island so as to have more sea room. *Otter* was a far cry from her former heyday of prewar times, when she had her fine coat of white and black, trimmed with green. She was dirty and unkempt, scarred and battered, and low in the water. She had aged a great deal in the past months. Even now Bob could see the bilge water being pumped over the side. The pumps had been kept going all the way to Cape Yakok from Adak Harbor, and from Cape Yakok to Ulak Island. In all likelihood they'd be worn out by the time *Otter* reached Dutch or Kodiak.

"What beats me," said Chuck MacIver conversationally, as he packed loose tobacco into a stubby pipe, "is that I never heard of any of the boys being out here at Ulak, eh, Bennie?"

Bennie shook his head. "Sure don't make sense, Chuck."

"Why not?" asked Gary. "Why not here at Ulak as well as any other of these godforsaken lumps of rock sticking up out of the sea in the middle of absolutely nowhere?"

Chuck lighted his pipe, waved out the match, then flipped it over the side. "Ask Bennie," he said between puffs.

The Scout shifted and looked at the island. "I can't say for sure," he said quietly. "I just know."

"He just knows," scoffed Gary.

Chuck nodded. "He knows," he said. He glanced at Bob. "You can bet on it. Besides, we usually know where the boys are. Never heard of any of them being here. Besides, what would the Japs be doing on Ulak?"

"Don't make sense," said Bennie.

Bob stood up and surveyed the shore. The cove mouth was narrow, but the cove widened within the arms of the entrance. A black beach showed, with a light surf running, nothing he couldn't handle. He had taken bigger boats into rougher waters than those many a time.

The Scouts were watching the shore as the boat eased into the cove. Gary Lunt kept his hand on the holstered Colt at his side, and if Bob hadn't been busy steering the boat, he'd have been doing the same thing. There was something chilling and repellent about the silent, brooding shores of Ulak Island.

The bows grounded. Bennie leaped out and waded ashore, taking the long bow painter with him. He made it

97

fast to an upthrust rock. Bob had dropped a light kedge anchor behind the boat as she had moved in to touch the shore, and the painter and anchor lines kept the boat bobbing easily in the light surf.

Chuck looked at Bob. " How do we do this? "

" This seems to be your department," said Bob.

Chuck nodded. " Me and Bennie will poke about. One of you lads can search along the shore. Better keep a guard on the boat. If anything happens, we'll fire three shots in rapid succession, and you'd better get out of here in a hurry. You never know."

" Yeh," said Gary hollowly. " You never know."

" What about you fellows? " asked Bob. " If we pull out, you'd be stranded here."

Bennie smiled. " I was born in these islands," he said. " Me and Chuck can get along, if the Nips don't clean our clocks for us, like Chuck always says. See you."

The two of them moved up a narrow-sided valley, and in a matter of minutes they had vanished from sight.

" You never know," repeated Gary. He shivered.

Bob climbed into the bows and dropped onto the beach.

" I'll take a look up and down the shore," he said. He withdrew the heavy automatic pistol from its holster and pulled back the slide, letting it snap forward to load the chamber. He slid up the safety and returned the pistol to the holster, tucking the flap up and then down into the area between the holster and the leather behind it to keep it out of the way.

He walked quickly along the beach, rounding an outthrust hill, to find himself looking along a wide beach at least a mile long, with no sign of life upon it or beyond the beach itself. He walked steadily on the wet black sand. A raven sailed over his head and turned inland cawing and croaking dismally. He eyed the water-bleached driftwood and the layers of kelp that covered much of the beach, hoping for a clue, but it was as if man had never set foot upon that lonely place.

Otter was out of sight. He looked toward the brooding hills and had the uncanny sensation that someone was watching him from up there. Fog swirled in from the sea and began to shroud the hills and in half an hour he was stalking through the gauzy opaqueness of it, with the hills and the sea hidden from him. His world was a small one of black sand and sea debris, not more than fifty or sixty feet in diameter.

Time and time again he stopped to listen, hearing nothing but the melancholy pounding of the surf farther up the beach and the sighing of the doleful wind. His footsteps were muffled in the soft wet sand, but even so, they seemed inordinately loud to him.

He saw a vague headland looming up through the cold, swirling fog and realized he had traversed that long, lonely beach. Bob stopped and tilted his head to one side, listening to wind and surf. The incredible cold loneliness of the place seemed to settle about him like an old and unwanted cloak. Fear came with the cloak, and the sudden impulse descended upon him to spin about and run like a frightened rabbit back to the boat and the companionship of Gary.

" Get ahold of yourself," he snapped aloud.

" Get ahold of yourself . . . get ahold of yourself . . . get ahold of yourself . . ." echoed the headland. The echo was ghostly and it shook Bob badly. Again he had the wild impulse to run. He placed his hand on the butt of the Colt, knowing full well it would be no protection at all against the unknown, and very little against a squad of tough

Japanese Marines, but it seemed to help.

He forced himself to walk around the towering head-land, with measured steps, until he had counted a hundred of them. He stopped and listened. Nothing but the wind and the surf. He turned and walked back, forcing himself to take the measured steps again, although the impulse descended on him over and over to take to his heels and run, run, run!

It seemed to Bob that he was walking for miles and miles in the dank and drifting fog and he wondered whether he might somehow have passed the boat and was walking far beyond it.

" Halt! " snapped a military-sounding voice, with a slight tremor in it. " Halt or I shoot! "

Bob croaked out a reply.

" Stand where you are! " rapped out the voice.

" It's me, you leadhead! " Bob cried.

" Advance one to be recognized! "

Bob rolled his eyes upward. " Oh, Lord," he breathed. " Give me strength! "

Gary sheathed his Colt. " Man, you gave me a start coming through the fog like that."

" How do you think I felt when you challenged me? "

" See anything? "

" Sea, surf, and sand, pal."

" Yeh." Gary rubbed his jaw. " How much longer do you think those Scouts will be poking around up there? "

" Not long," said a quiet voice out of the fog not twenty feet from them. " Don't reach for those peashooters, boys. Bennie's covering you from the other side."

Gary grinned weakly. " I'm glad you boys are on our side," he said.

Chuck MacIver came out of the fog and grounded his

rifle. " Good thing we are," he said dryly. " Otherwise you would be dead by now. Me and Bennie could hear you half a mile off. Fog carries noise. Better remember that if you plan to enjoy your visit to these islands very long."

" Yup," said Bennie. He shoved back his parka hood. " Not a blessed soul on this island."

Chuck filled his pipe and lighted it. " I told you Bennie was right," he said. " Coulda saved us a long walk. No sign of anyone, Scouts *or* Japs. You sure your uncle got that message right, Bob? "

Bob nodded. " I read it before he filed it away. It said Ulak, all right."

" And the Scouts were supposed to have been alerted by radio, eh? "

" Yes."

" Beats me," said Chuck.

" They were never here," said Bennie matter-of-factly. He peeled the cover from a candy bar and broke the bar into three pieces in his big hands, giving Bob and Gary a share of the sweet. " Chuck, he don't like candy," he added. " All the time that lousy pipe. Whoeee! Seems like a Jap could smell that thing a mile away."

Bob chewed the somewhat stale candy. " I suppose we'll have to go back to the *Otter*," he said. " You're sure you couldn't have missed them, Chuck? "

" Positive." Chuck raised his rifle and flipped over the safety catch. He raised the rifle and fired once, threw the bolt, fired again, then once more. The crashing reports echoed strongly from the hills and fled along the beach to die away. " Don't get excited, fellows," said Chuck. " I told your uncle I'd signal that way and twice more if we were to leave the island in fog. There aren't any Japs around to hear it."

101

"Not unless they have a sub offshore," said Bob.

Chuck's eyes widened. "I never thought of that."

"Too late now," said Gary.

Bennie raised his head. "Wind will shift," he stated. "Get stronger. Can't waste much time here or we'll never get back to the boat."

Twenty minutes passed. Chuck fired three times. The echoes died away to be replaced by the sound of the surf and wind.

"Wind will shift," said Gary. He grinned. "Bennie the weather seer."

At that very moment the wind died away and a moment later it shifted, and shifted again, blowing from the land out to sea, tattering the fog veils and driving them out to sea, revealing the nakedness of the gray-green hills.

"Yup," said Chuck as he reloaded his rifle. "Bennie the ol' weather seer."

"Sea coming up," said Bennie. "Time to shove off."

Gary darted up the beach and released the painter.

Chuck grinned. "You got a rep now with ol' Gary, Bennie," he said.

Bennie grinned along with Chuck. "All I do is guess," he said.

"Yeh," said Bob. "You sure do."

The three of them shoved the boat into the surf. Gary followed them over the bows. Bob turned the boat away from the inhospitable shore and steered almost by sound, listening to the beating of the waves on either hand as the boat passed through the cove entrance and plunged out toward the open sea, taking spray over the bows. Gary rigged the canvas weather dodger up forward to keep the boat from getting swamped.

Half an hour passed and there was no sight or sound of

Otter. Bob stared into the thick wreathing fog. The seas were rising and the wind was getting a shriek to it.

Chuck fired three times into the fog overhead. The harsh sound of the shooting died away to be replaced by the whispering of the water against the sides of the boat and the eldritch shrieking of the wind.

Bennie shifted on his thwart. He pointed off the port bow. " That way, kid," he said.

Five minutes later the boat came alongside the pitching *Otter.* Her sails were set and she was heeling more than she should have been. The boat was hooked on to the falls and hoisted dripping from the sea. She was lowered into the chocks and lashed fast.

" Nothing, Skipper," said Bob. " Not a sight or a sound."

Mack shook his head. " Something's wrong. Well, if they weren't there, they weren't there."

" Now for home! " said Gary.

Mack shook his head again. " The engine quit completely on us," he said quietly. " We'll have to run before the wind, using the sails until Jim and Thor can get the diesel in running order. Get set for a rough night, boys."

Even as he spoke, the wind arose in pitch, driving hard and cold from almost due east, slamming great gray-green seas hard against the battered sides of the *Otter,* as she fled westward before the fury of the storm, toward the distant island of Amchitka, perhaps seventy-five miles away. Beyond Amchitka was Rat Island, Little Sitkin, Chugul, and Little Kiska, and beyond Little Kiska, farther west, was Kiska itself, the closest Japanese base to American-held Adak, now almost a hundred miles behind *Otter* as she moved, almost helplessly, farther and farther west into the cold and clinging fog.

9

Iɴ ᴛʜᴇ howling maelstrom of the winter night, *Otter* was taking the worst beating of her career. A man could hardly see his hand held at arm's length in front of his face. Alternate blasts of icy rain and stinging snow swept across the dark turmoil of the heaving seas. She drove on to the unknown west under a working jib and her mizzen sail, triple-reefed, hardly more than pocket handkerchiefs in size, but they served to steady her. There were times when it appeared as though she'd go down altogether when she slid down the long liquid slopes after laboriously crawling up the seemingly mountainous crests.

A man could not stay on his feet within the shelter of the superstructure. The pitching decks were a mess of broken crockery, trampled food, soaked clothing, and reeking vomit, for hardly a man had not succumbed to the wild gyrations of the little vessel as she gamely fought for her life in the worst seas Mack Dunbar admitted he had ever seen in those waters.

The pumps were still working, hardly keeping even with the inflow of the icy water through the split seams and unseen leaks in the once almost watertight hull of *Otter*. The bilge water was no longer dirty; it was clean sea water. That in itself was a warning that *Otter* was leaking dangerously.

In the little engine room Thor Andreason and Jim Brannon still worked over the engine, although at times they were pitched helplessly from one end of the engine room to the other. Jim was bleeding from a deep gash over one bushy eyebrow. Tools and parts clattered back and forth beneath their feet as they worked.

Baldy's galley was in complete chaos. There had been no hot food for twelve hours, and in all likelihood there would be none within the next twelve hours unless the storm blew itself out or *Otter* outran it, which was hardly likely. It was a question of grinning and bearing it.

Every opening that might admit the icy seas was tightly sealed, but even so the water worked its way in, running inches deep along the companionways, pouring down the ladders, sloshing about in the bilges.

The pilothouse at times was a little island in a whirling mass of water and spray as *Otter* swung down deeply, hardly trying to throw off the seas, almost welcoming them aboard rather than having to fight them off. The helmsman was lashed to the wheel. Half of the windows had been smashed and boarded up, and water slopped back and forth on the deck.

Otter shuddered and pitched, wallowed and swayed, rose and fell in a mad rigadoon danced to the eldritch cacophony of the wind. The sea and wind were striking to disable, then maim, then kill. There would be no quarter given that wild night. It was a fight to the death, and the odds were with King Weather.

Otter wasn't moving because of the impetus of the weathered and patched scraps of sail, but rather because of the driving scend of the huge seas, and somewhere ahead of her, unseen in the unknown distance, was the great long island of Amchitka, with but one fair harbor for the whole area of the island. If *Otter* missed Constantine Harbor, she'd drive ashore on the rocks and black sand, and the battering seas would smash her and her motley crew and passengers into bloody pulp in the grinding surf. If, by a fluke, she missed the long island altogether, she would drive on and on into the western seas into the icy oblivion of hell-lashed waters.

She rolled. How she rolled! It was a frightening and sickening motion in the cross seas as she shuddered her way through them. It was impossible for her to keep afloat, but she did so.

Bob Dunbar hung on to the wheel, watching the gyrations of the compass card. No course could be held. All he could do was try to ease the gallant little cockleshell as she fought her lone battle against the sea and the wind. He had been at the wheel of the vessel for an hour and it seemed like ten. If *Otter* broached to, it would be the end of her. She'd never survive if the waves came at her over the side. The phrase *spurlos versenkt* came back to Bob. *Spurlos versenkt;* sunk without trace. Perhaps a fragment of the vessel would drift ashore on some uninhabited island, perhaps never to be seen through eternity by the eyes of men.

Mack Dunbar risked poking his head out of the door to check the sails. He ducked back in again as almost solid spray crashed against the side of the pilothouse. " They're holding," he said. He looked at the wind-speed needle flickering across its dial, motivated by the wind cups of the anemometer whirling at frantic speed in the invisible clutch of the wind. " Force Ten," he said at last.

Bob swallowed hard. Force Ten on the Beaufort Wind Scale was listed as a Whole Gale, wind speeds 55 to 63 miles per hour. Force Eleven was a Storm, wind speeds

64 to 75 miles per hour, and beyond that was Force Twelve, Hurricane, above 75 miles per hour.

"We might be able to see by dawn," said his uncle. "If we don't —"

There was no need for him to continue. No one could see through the darkness of the night and the gale to spot the island that was somewhere ahead of them in the howling rack. There would be little if any warning before *Otter* drove onto the cruel shore to smash her wooden bones to pulpwood. They had no idea where *Otter* was at the moment. It would be a race between hitting the island and greeting the cold and gray dawn light. Even so, there was little hope that *Otter* would ever be able to match the seas on her way back east unless her hull was calked and her engine was in good running order.

"Ulak," said Mack Dunbar.

Bob glanced at him.

There was an odd look in his uncle's eyes. He had taken the water-wrinkled radio form from the little filing cabinet bolted to the after wall. He was studying it closely. He reached into a drawer, bracing himself between the wall and the chart table. He held a magnifying glass in one huge hand while he studied the form.

"What do you mean, Skipper?" asked Bob.

Mack Dunbar looked up. "The writing was sloppy in the first place," he said quietly, "and the seawater didn't help much. As far as I can make it out, this word isn't Ulak at all, but rather Omak Island, *east* of Adak, and not more than ten miles from it. Kid, *we came the wrong way from Cape Yakok.*"

Otter shuddered in the merciless watery grip of the seas.

"If I had read the message right," said Mack Dunbar, "we'd have had those Scouts off of Omak, and would have

107

been well on the way to Dutch by now. Instead, we're being driven westward, in danger of foundering or running ashore on Amchitka — all because I made the mistake of not interpreting that message correctly."

Bob turned back to look at the compass, although it did little good. "No use crying about it," he said quietly. "Our job now is to save *Otter* and the men aboard her."

There was no answer from Mack Dunbar, but a moment later a big hand clamped itself on Bob's right shoulder. "Right, kid," said Mack. "I almost forgot my duty. Thanks, Bob. I needed a kick in the jeans to get my spirits back."

"We can work her into a cove on Amchitka," said Bob, "and maybe beach her at low tide, long enough to give her some temporary calking, refloat her, and work on the engine until it's running good enough to get us back. Meanwhile we can work out extra sails from the tarpaulins we have in the hold and with their help we can get back east."

"Never say die, eh?"

"You have the general idea," said Bob with a grin.

"Out of the mouths of babes," said Mack. "We'll make a sailor out of you yet, kid."

"Look!" said Bob.

Faintly to the east, hardly distinguishable in the flying scud, was the faintest trace of pewter light. The dawn had won the race against the cruel shore of Amchitka.

Mack Dunbar smiled, then as quickly as the smile had come, it faded from his face and his square jaw tightened. He was gazing steadfastly off the port bow of the vessel. Bob turned to see what his uncle was looking at and a cold chill flowed through his body. There, not half a mile away, was a bold headland, wreathed in tendrils of drifting fog, while at its base, deepest in the sea, breakers curled and smashed, venting their fury on the solid rock.

Mack Dunbar wasted no time. " All hands on deck! " he roared. He practically leaped out on the starboard wing of the bridge, and as the crew boiled up from below, some of them half dressed, he rapped out his commands with the precision of an automatic weapon. *Otter* slowly, ever so slowly, came about and slanted away from that menacing shore, but to Bob Dunbar, still at the helm, it seemed as though the battle was lost and that wind and tide were playing with *Otter* like a cat plays with a mouse. The small patches of sail were stiff as sheets of metal and the shrouds and lines were drawn ringing hard as the wind, baffled in its attempt to pile *Otter* ashore, was now trying to blow the canvas from the bolt ropes to make her completely helpless.

There was nothing for the men aboard to do but stand at the lee rail and watch that bold and dominering head-land waiting for the wooden bones of *Otter* and the flesh and bones of the men aboard her. In a matter of minutes Mack Dunbar would have to make his decision to stay with his ship or abandon her for the small boats, and even then there might not be a chance to clear the headland. With that sea running and the whining of the wind beating toward the land, the small boats would hardly have more of a chance than *Otter*.

Mack opened the pilothouse door. " Thank God the wind eased off a little in the past twenty minutes."

" Do you recognize that headland, Skipper? "

" I think it's East Cape."

Bob could hardly muster enough courage to ask his next question. " Where? " he finally blurted.

" Amchitka, kid. We're a long, long way from home. If the Japs are ashore there, they can hardly miss us. I doubt if they have an airfield built there. Our intelligence reports from submarine and air reconnaissance indicate they might be on Amchitka, but not in strength, at least not enough to build an airfield. But they might have seaplanes or floatplanes. Perhaps a sub or two. Maybe even some surface craft."

Bob smiled wanly. " That's all we need."

As *Otter* struggled for a little sea room, there was no indication that the Japanese were on Amchitka, which didn't mean a thing. They could watch out to sea and never be seen. The fog was tattered by the wind, and slowly, ever so slowly, *Otter* fought her way into a thick patch of it, trying to round East Cape.

" Where is Constantine Harbor? " asked Bob.

Mack pointed astern. " Around East Cape. We can't make it in this wind and sea, kid. Besides, I'm not so sure I want to use Constantine. It's a natural for the Japs to scout it now and then looking for American ships or troops. Remember, we're only about sixty miles or so from Kiska."

Mack began to fill his pipe. " We have only one choice. To work our way up the south coast of Amchitka and look for a cove where we can work on *Otter*. That won't be easy. I've been here before, but only in Constantine Harbor."

" What if they find us? " asked Bob.

Mack lighted his pipe. " We can go ashore and hide out. We've got guns. We can use 'em."

" Can't we radio for help? "

" We could, but I don't want to break radio silence at this time."

" It's like sitting on the doorstep of a lion's den, hoping he won't stumble over you."

" You've got the general idea, kid."

As the sky lightened above the flying clouds *Otter*

110

worked her way slowly, with hardly more than steerage-way, around frowning East Cape and along the hostile south shore. Every man aboard, except Jim Brannon and Thor Andreason who were still slaving over the stubborn engine, scanned the shore for signs of a cove where *Otter* could take shelter. If the gale died away, there would be a chance that seaplanes might scout the island. The Japanese were known to have such craft at Kiska. *Mavis* was the American code name given to the Kawanishi 97 patrol bombers that had been observed in the air and also in Kiska Harbor. Recently smaller floatplanes had been spotted, the excellent single-seater Zero, or Mitsubishi 52 Type " 0," nicknamed *"Zeke"* if it was used as a land or carrier plane, *" Rufe "* if it was equipped with floats. *Rufes* would be used in the Aleutians because of the lack of Japanese airfields on Kiska and Attu. It was said about them that they had remarkable maneuverability, which was unusual in a floatplane. Reports indicated that *Rufe* was well armed with two 7.7mm. machine guns mounted in the fuselage and two 20mm. guns in the wings. *Rufe* had also been known to carry small bombs beneath the wings. It wouldn't take much of a bombing and strafing to put *Otter* under the water.

Even with the possible threat of Japanese planes in those lonely waters there was another threat that was more sinister, to Bob's way of thinking, at any rate. He had never forgotten seeing the enemy sub off Kagalaska in early September. Only by the grace of God had *Otter* been saved from instant destruction. He still shivered a little when he remembered the black muzzle of the sub's deck gun as it had been trained on *Otter* while the sub sped after the small vessel.

" Man those guns! " commanded Mack Dunbar. It was

111

almost as though he had been reading Bob's mind.

Mike Pucci and Smitty uncovered the 20mm. gun, cocked and loaded it, shielding it from flying spray by loosely tying the canvas cover about it once it was ready for action. Jesse Easter was still pale-faced, for the Arkansas boy had never been able to overcome his sea-sickness, although he had managed somehow to learn to live with it.

The rest of the men, with the exception of Baldy, the cook, and Thor and Jim, lined the rails of the little craft, armed with rifles. Mack Dunbar took a Springfield rifle from the rack in the pilothouse and loaded it. He swung a web pistol belt about his waist, heavy with holstered automatic pistol and filled clip pouch. He buckled another pistol belt about Bob's slim waist. " You never know," he said quietly.

Otter wallowed along until suddenly the seas seemed calmer, and Bob realized they had passed from the area where the wind had its greatest strength behind the shelter of the very cape that had been such a menace, thus revers-ing its role from menace to protector. Still it would be touch and go in those dangerous, poorly charted waters. Even under power the vessel would have been in a tough situation. Under canvas the odds against her making the shelter of a cove, *if* a cove existed, were almost insur-mountable.

Mack Dunbar scanned the forbidding shore with his binoculars, shaking his head from time to time. " Now and then I think I see an opening into a cove, but I'm not sure. I can't take the old girl into those waters and chance ripping out her bottom on rocks."

Bob eased the helm a little. " Let me take the powerboat inshore, Skipper. We can take soundings."

" No! Too dangerous! "

" It's more dangerous to drift along out here, Skipper."

There was no argument forthcoming from Mack Dunbar. The powerboat was lowered into the heaving seas, and Gary Lunt, Chuck MacIver, and Bennie Dutton joined Bob in the boat. The falls were cast loose, the boat fended off and turned toward shore, plunging and wallowing in the heavy seas, spray flying up in icy showers, dashing against the canvas dodger, pouring into the little boat now and then as she put alternate gunwales under a wave. The three passengers bailed steadily as Bob eased the boat closer into the smoother water, eyeing the battering surf that creamed against the naked black rock of the shore.

The powerboat entered an area where the seas were greasy-looking but were not breaking. Here and there a rock showed itself by its cap of frothing white spray. Bob looked ahead. He thought he saw an opening in the rocky shore, but as they drew closer he saw that he was mistaken. A craggy headland, naked of vegetation, thrust itself boldly out into the sea. As the powerboat rounded it, Bennie Dutton pointed toward the inner side of the headland with his dripping bailing can. It looked as though there was a cove or inlet beyond the outer edge of the headland, almost fully concealed by overhanging rock that looked as though it was ready to fall at a touch.

Gary Lunt coiled his lead line as Bob throttled down until the powerboat was barely making steerageway. Gary swung out the lead with practiced ease, and as the boat moved up on it he lifted it and lowered it, feeling for the bottom. " No bottom," he called out.

The boat crept in toward the looming headland. A naked pinnacle of sharp-edged rock showed ten yards off the port bow.

113

"By the mark thirteen," called Gary.

"Seventy-eight feet," said Bob to Chuck MacIver.

"By the mark twelve! By the mark twelve! By the mark twelve!" chanted Gary. "Feels like sand bottom. Mark underwater, eleven! Mark underwater, eleven! And a half, ten! By the mark ten!"

The headland was close enough for Bob to hit it with a rock, and on the opposite, or port, side, a long arm of rocky formation reached out for them as they inched in toward rougher water curling about the fanged rock.

"And a half, nine! By the mark nine! Sand bottom!" called Gary.

Bob gave the motor a little more throttle and glanced astern. The *Otter* was out of sight. He looked ahead again. Nowhere ahead of them, at least within fifty yards, could he see an opening into the rock wall that towered above the little boat like the grim facade of some impregnable medieval castle.

"Mark underwater, eight! By the mark eight! By the mark seven! Shoaling fast!" chanted Gary.

"Look," said Bennie Dutton quietly. He pointed astern.

Bob risked a backward glance and his stomach flipped over. *Otter* was plainly in sight, beating in toward the headland under her taut scraps of sail, plunging and rising, plunging and rising in the heavy seas. What was wrong with the skipper?

"By the mark six! By the mark five underwater!"

Bob looked ahead, then astern, and it seemed to him that *Otter* was moving faster than she had been for many hours, footing steadily along with a ragged scarf of water being pushed ahead of her by her blunt and scarred bows.

"Is he outa his mind?" growled Bennie.

"By the mark five underwater! Sand bottom! And a half,

114

four! By the deep three! Shoaling almighty fast! "

Bob looked up at the headland. A gull sailed out of a crevice, swooping low over the boat. The wash of the seas in that confined space had a deadly, menacing sound. It gurgled and slobbered into the openings and fell back, concealing rocks just below, or at the surface.

" By the mark three! "

Eighteen feet of water beneath the boat. Bob glanced ahead. It seemed as though there was an opening there, hardly more than fifty feet wide.

" By the mark two! By the mark two! By the mark two! Mark one and a half! Look ahead! " called Gary.

Bob looked up. The rock walls seemed to draw apart from each other, showing a wide cove beyond, hemmed in by towering walls, with a desolate black sand beach strewn with kelp like the long hair of a drowned woman.

" By the mark two! And a half, three! By the mark three! And a half, four! By the mark five! By the mark five! By the mark six underwater! By the mark seven! "

" Pull in your line," snapped Bob. He gave the boat more power and swung her within the deep well of the hidden cove, steering for the entrance. The boat shot past the rock wall on the portside and toward the more open water, to see *Otter* not two hundred yards away.

There was some reason why Mack Dunbar was risking *Otter* that close in unknown waters. *Otter* neared the land. Men stood by her sails. Mack Dunbar stood on the starboard wing of the bridge, staring toward land.

" Wave him on," said Bob. " God help us if we're wrong! He'll never get off again now. He *has* to make the cove! "

Bob turned the boat and steered up the channel, casting backward glances at *Otter* as she neared the dangerous headland. She was too wide for the entrance, thought Bob, then knew he was wrong, for the entrance only looked that way. Even so, it would be a narrow squeak with no chance to maneuver under sail.

Otter raised to meet the surf, drove on, swept by tide as well as wind. She was coming in like a surfboard. Now she was in the entrance. Bob steered the powerboat to starboard and stood up, shouting and waving, pointing toward the seemingly solid wall that hid the narrow mouth of the inner cove. Mack Dunbar, pipe thrust out from his square jaw, nodded as coolly as though he was coming into Kodiak or Dutch.

Otter shot past the powerboat. The sails were dropped at Mack's command. She cruelly scraped the rock wall to starboard, leaving great splinters of her wooden flesh hanging in the fangs of the cliff. Bob poured on the power and shot after the *Otter*. She was in the inner cove heading for the beach.

" Let fall forward! " roared Mack Dunbar. " Let fall aft! "

The bow and stern anchors plunged into the cold, dark waters and *Otter* surged forward, then back again as the hooks sank into the sandy bottom. She was safe from the sea, but if her engine was not repaired she'd never get out of that cove under sail.

Bob brought the powerboat alongside *Otter* and Gary secured her by her bow painter. Bob looked up at his uncle and at the white-faced men on the decks. " Couldn't you have waited a little? " he said dryly.

Mack Dunbar lighted his pipe. " Listen," he said quietly. He thrust a stubby thumb upward.

Faintly, above the steady washing of the sea, and the doleful moaning of the wind about the towering rock walls, came a droning sound.

Bob looked up. High in the sky, below a cloud layer, he saw a silvery airplane moving inland — a small, swift-looking plane with a long float beneath her fuselage, extending far beyond her radial engine. As the plane tilted and banked, he saw red circles beneath the wings. His throat went dry and his heart thudded hard against his ribs. There was no mistaking the type. It was a float Zero, a *Rufe!*

Mack flipped the match over the side. "Now you know why we couldn't stay out there like a sitting duck. If he'd have spotted us —"

Chuck MacIver spat over the side. "Pontoon Joe," he said dryly.

The plane vanished, leaving the sound of its engine behind it. Soon that faded away as well.

Mack looked down at his motley crew. "You men know the score," he said. "We can't move out of here until we get the engine fixed. Even at that, we'll have to beach *Otter* and patch some of the leaks in her hull before we try those seas again. Any of you who want to leave now and hide out on land, go ahead and do so."

Not a man moved.

As they set to work they could hear the distant droning of Pontoon Joe as he scouted the island.

10

THE night had fallen with northern swiftness, but still the crew of *Otter,* as well as the Army men aboard, worked on in a race against time. She had been moved into shallower water and beached, with mooring lines made fast to deeply embedded rocks on the dark shore. Everything that could be removed from the vessel, except her stores of fuel oil, had been taken ashore either by floating or in the small boats. Even the fresh-water tanks had been drained, for one of the few blessings of the Aleutians was the fact that fresh water was always available in great quantities from melting snow and the constant rains.

The vessel sat with her blunt nose resting on the black sands, fair target for the enemy. If they found *Otter* in her hideout, she'd never survive. One advantage *Otter* had was that the sheer walls protected her from a direct bombing raid, and also from sight unless a pilot or observer happened to look straight down into the gigantic pothole in which *Otter* was hidden. It wasn't too much comfort, but it was better than being out on the open sea, or on an exposed beach. One other advantage, and perhaps the best of the two, was that Baldy was able to get his galley cleaned up and in business, for hot food and drink are like precious gems in the Aleutians. Baldy even issued vitamin pills from some hidden store of his own. They would be needed . . .

Thor Andreason and Jim Brannon were still at work. Vital parts were needed, and the two engineers were hard put to figure out how to get around the need, but they kept on working while *Otter* was beached. Somehow or other the twenty millimeter gun was unbolted from the foredeck, disassembled, and then raised by the main boom and lowered into the powerboat. It was taken ashore and man-handled to the sand. With the aid of poles beneath it, it was carried to a rock shelf overlooking the entrance to the cove, and with a fair view of the open sea. Here Mike Pucci and Smitty worked until they had the gun well em-placed behind a rock barricade with a good field of fire. The gun would be no match for the heavy deck gun of a Japanese submarine, but it could prevent landing parties from entering the cove. If they elected to land elsewhere and come overland to reach the cove from the rear, the gun could do nothing to stop them.

The fifty caliber Army machine gun was left on the afterdeck with a better field of fire now that the small boats were kept in the water. Some of the running rigging had been dropped to the decks for repairs, and if Jesse Easter shot away the standing rigging in defense of *Otter*, it couldn't be helped. The standing rigging could always be replaced. The machine gun also could cover the inner entrance to the cove, though it could not fire toward much of the beach because of the defilade of the funnel, mizzen-mast, and pilothouse. It could cover the approach of an enemy plane if it elected to come down dangerously close to the huge pothole, which was hardly likely.

The tide would have to run out before *Otter*'s hull could be fully checked and temporarily calked. Meanwhile it was necessary to scout the surrounding terrain. Bob, Gary, Bennie Dutton, and Chuck MacIver volunteered to go.

Armed with rifles and pistols, a grenade or two, and heavy sheath knives, the four of them worked their way up the treacherous cliff face in the darkness. The wind had weakened greatly, but now and then gusts swept into the cove with harrowing force and the quartet clung to the cliff face like limpets to a rock. It took them an hour to reach the lip of the rock wall, and they rolled over onto the matted, damp tundra that covered the cliff top like a moldy toupee and lay there to regain their breath and strength.

It was not as dark atop the cliff as it was in the cove far below them. A vague, indefinite light flowed with spectral appearance across the mossy-looking tundra, while the deep valleys that flowed away from the higher land were deep in menacing shadow. Here and there were dark, curving lines on the gray-green of the slopes that indicated semisubterranean streams that had cut their way through tundra and black mud, down to the bedrock, while the tundra had overgrown the upper edges of the twisted channels like lank uncut hair. Bare as the land seemed to be, there were many places where a man could hide with ease in deep hollows, or the beds of streams, or among some of the black rock formations that thrust themselves up through the layer of mud and tundra like dislocated ebony bones.

It was Bennie Dutton who led the way down the slope, his shoe pacs sinking ankle-deep into the tundra with a sucking sound. As they walked, the foot holes slowly began to fill with subsurface water. They skirted tiny ponds and miniature lakes, hardly more than a few inches to several feet deep, of clear cold water, pleasant to the taste.

Bob Dunbar carried his Springfield rifle in the crook of his left arm, cocked with the thumb safety on, while his Colt was also cocked and swung heavily at his side. Both

Bob and Gary were experienced with firearms, for Bob and Gary had often accompanied their fathers on deer- and bear-hunting trips on the mainland. He took up the rear as Bennie led the way. The half-breed Aleut tested the night with his senses, like a questing hound, and Chuck MacIver, who had spent the past ten years of his life trapping and hunting, fishing and exploring the Aleutian Chain from Unimak to Gareloi, was hardly less alert.

There was no chance that a Japanese plane would be reconnoitering at night, but dawn might tell another story. A quartet of men could easily hide from the prying eyes of an enemy flyer, but *Otter* could hardly be hidden that well. The enemy would be keeping an eye on Amchitka, for it was the most logical place for the Americans to establish their next base in the leapfrogging movement west, closer and closer to Kiska and Attu. *The Japanese might even now be established on Amchitka!* The chilling thought lanced through Bob as he plodded on through the soft, tiring tundra. He began to look at each hummock and hill with suspicious eyes.

The wind was fitful, playing about as though tired of the vast effort it had put out to sink *Otter*, and was now like a small boy who knows he has lost his fight and yet is reluctant to leave lest he lose face before his jeering friends. When almost unexpectedly it died away, a great quietness fell over the long, empty-looking island, with nothing but the distant murmuring of the surf to break the silence of the night.

Far over the humped, sleeping shapes of the hills, past a hunched and almost indistinct mountain, something was forming mysteriously in the night. Bob narrowed his eyes. Then he knew it for what it was — a long, raggedy tendril of approaching fog. It was rolling down the slope of the

121

mountain toward a deep valley. Soon only the rounded top of the mountain showed above the shifting, swiftly moving veil of fog. Slowly the fog began to rise, blotting out the entire mountain, and at a rapid pace it flowed down into the valley, hiding it from view and began a stealthy and utterly silent approach toward the four men.

More and more fog billowed in from the sea impelled by the fitful offshore wind. The fog was three thousand to four thousand feet deep, a thick, almost impenetrable barrier to sight, and a deceptive carrier of sound. Almost before he realized it, Bob was padding across the squelching tundra with the first damp fingers of the fog touching his face and hands. Since the first appearance of the fog around the distant mountain, it had taken exactly nineteen minutes, timed by Bob's wristwatch, to travel the entire width of the island, blotting it out completely.

Chuck MacIver turned to look at Bob. " Well, anyway, it will keep the Jap flyers grounded and keep *Otter* concealed."

" 'Thank God from whom all blessings flow,' " said Bennie. He shifted his rifle and looked about. He raised his head and listened. " Let's work over to the left, closer to the shore. I don't need to tell you fellows to watch out you don't walk over a cliff brink. That first step can be a nasty one! "

In an hour they had reached a point not far to the west of the cove where *Otter* lay hidden. Just at their feet was the brink of a cliff and below the brink was nothing but a thick, drifting blanket of fog like grayish cotton batting. It seemed almost as though one could walk upon it. Far below them they could hear the muted crashing of the cold seas upon the rocky shore.

Bennie grounded his camouflaged rifle. " You guys want

122

to take a rest while I poke around?"

Chuck shook his head. "I'll go with you, Bennie," he said. "We've been together through these islands. I'm not going to let you wander off by yourself. You boys stick tight here. We won't lose you." He followed Bennie off into the fog.

Gary dropped flat on the damp tundra. "Man," he said, "being at sea sure takes away your land legs. I thought that crazy Aleut planned to walk clear to the other end of the island."

"Me too," said Bob. "I'll swear he's got web feet."

"I think they were laughing at us."

Bob shrugged. "Let 'em," he said.

The fog shifted and wavered, flowing along the lip of the cliff. Gary dropped on his stomach and edged out to the very brink, looking down toward the sea. It was like looking into a gray malted milk. Slowly, almost imperceptibly, he began to see hunched rock shapes, and now and again the sea as it rose and smashed itself against the rocks. He felt sure he was looking down in a large cove. When he could see through the fog, a dim and indistinct line seemed to be a curved continuation of the brink upon which he and Gary were resting.

He looked down again and could see the surface of the water within the cove, with drifting veils of fog crossing it. Suddenly he saw something else and his eyes widened — something long and narrow, almost awash, with a tower-like protuberance thrusting itself up from the rounded back of the long shape. He stared at it. The fog enveloped it, and he was sure he had been imagining things. He glanced at Gary. Gary was flat on his back with a wisp of grass in his mouth, staring up into the opaqueness above him.

Bob inched forward and looked down again. The fog swirled and lifted, fell and swirled, in twisting shapes that looked oddly like gauzy veils whipped by the wind. Now the fog cleared and he could see the water once again. This time he was sure. He was looking down on a Japanese type submarine, for he knew American types well enough. This was no fleet type submarine or smaller S boat, as used by the United States Navy in those waters.

Gary shifted lazily. " Man, I sure could use a double hamburger with fries and a double thick malted from Charlie's place in Anchorage," he said. " How 'bout you? "

Bob watched the submarine fade into the thick fog. " Quiet! " Bob ordered.

" You trying to sleep? "

Bob reached over and gripped Gary by the arm. " Shut up! " he said. " Look down there! "

Gary rolled over and came up beside Bob. " Nothing but fog, fog, and more fog," he said. " You gone Aleutian-happy, bub? You got the ol' Aleutian stare, kid? "

" Look again! "

" I still think — " Gary's voice trailed away. " Jumpin' Jehosephat! " He stared at the submarine and then looked at Bob. " One of ours? "

Bob shook his head.

" You sure? "

" Positive."

Gary rubbed his dirty face. " Doesn't seem to be anyone around it." He eyed Bob. " You don't suppose it's been abandoned? "

" Who knows? There's one sure way to find out."

Gary smiled weakly. " Now, how did I know you were going to say that? "

" Intuition."

"But why find out?"

Bob hitched his rifle up beside him. "Subs have diesel engines for running on the surface — even Jap subs. *Otter* has a diesel engine. Maybe we could cannibalize enough parts off of that one to repair *Otter's* diesel."

"Brilliant," said Gary dryly. "We know a lot about diesels, don't we? Maybe we can get an itemized list of parts from the Jap sub and take it back to Jim Brannon."

Bob slid his feet over the edge of the cliff and felt for a hold as he slung his rifle cross his back. "There are two things we have to know: First, is it abandoned? Second, are her diesels underwater or completely damaged if she *is* abandoned? It's as simple as that."

"Yeh. Heh-heh-heh — "

"You want to stay on this drowned mountaintop for the rest of your life, or until the Japs come and carve you up with a samurai sword?" said Bob fiercely.

"No."

"Then come on, Windy Willie!" Bob slid down to a ledge and began to work his way down the cliff face. The fog swirled about him as he did so. It was like feeling one's way down into a well full of thick smoke. His feet met narrow ledges of rock, and quite often a questing foot would fan nothing but air. The fog swirled away and he found himself standing on a ledge, hardly more than a foot wide, with no way, to the eye, at any rate, to descend farther. As the fog cleared he could see the sheer face of the cliff falling away below him to a spiked bed of rock littering the narrow black beach. He looked up to see Gary's legs probing for a hold above him. There was nothing to do but try to find a way down, and he knew they'd have to find a way down, for it would be impossible to ascend again the way they had come.

125

Inch by inch he probed into the face of the cliff with his toes, gripping his hands into crevices, while his bulky parka impeded his progress and his pistol belt snagged points of rock. He did not dare look down. The fog swirled away. If a Japanese came out on the deck of that submarine and looked up, he could not miss seeing the two boys plastered against the face of the cliff, like flies in amber.

His face was hard against the cliff and his fingers were bleeding while his toes dug frantically at the cliff face for a minute hold. A piece of rock fell from above him and struck him cruelly atop his parka hood. He hung on while his senses swirled like the fog, then forced himself to work lower and lower, not daring to look down. Once again the fog crept in and he could see neither up nor down. There was nothing to do but keep working down the cliff face. Minutes later his left foot slipped, his right scrabbled for a hold, while his hands slipped, and just as he thought he was going to fall he felt cold water wash up around his shoe pacs and he knew he had reached the unseen beach.

He quickly unslung his rifle and held it at his waist, peering through the fog, trying to see the sub. Gary's feet thudded on the beach. A moment later icy seawater washed up about their knees. Bob shivered as he waded toward the area where he had seen the sub. The fog swirled away and he saw that the beach widened. He saw something else. The faint marks of feet and of wheels. Driftwood boards had been laid upon the soft sand so that the wheels might not sink in too deeply. He walked softly toward the cliff face, following the tracks. The tracks vanished into a dark-looking cave that drove into the living rock itself. He stopped and waved Gary back, then he trotted back and the two of them sank down behind a rock dike that thrust itself up through the sand.

They waited there for five minutes, listening to the swashing of the surf and the faint voice of the wind. Bob got to his feet, and scared as he was, he walked forward in the mingled foot and wheel tracks until he reached the mouth of that uninviting cave. There he saw faint light at the far end of it, but no sight or sound of life in the cave. He walked in softly, flipping off the safety catch of his rifle. The tracks continued on, and when he reached the end of the cave he saw that it opened into a narrow walled valley that slanted steeply upward toward the top of the cliff with a trickle of water running down it. On both sides of the trickle were deep-set foot and wheel tracks as though men had struggled to drag something up that valley to the plateau high above the cove.

" What do you think? " whispered Gary hoarsely from behind Bob.

" Jap landing party," said Bob in a low voice.

" You sure? "

" What else could it be? " Bob turned on a heel, and as he did so he saw something leaning against the side of the cave. He walked to it and saw that it was a rifle, but not of a type with which he was familiar. He leaned his own rifle against the wall and picked up the strange rifle. It was shaped something like the familiar Springfield Model 1903 that he carried, but had a rounded pistol grip, and the butt stock was made of two pieces. The sling was made of canvas, covered with a rubbery-looking material, and was on the left side of the rifle rather than beneath it, like the Springfield. The knob at the end of the bolt handle was pear-shaped, and the bolt handle awkwardly thrust itself out at right angles to the bolt instead of being turned down. He examined the breech as well as he could in the darkness and knew as he traced the stamping above the chamber that he was holding a Japanese rifle, an Arisaka, for the Government stamping on the metal was that of a chrysanthemum, with curious letters below the gas escape port.

"Well?" whispered Gary.

"Jap rifle," said Bob.

"Coulda been here a long time."

"Not from the looks of it. One of them must have left it here while helping get whatever they were moving, up that valley."

"Yeh, and he might be on his way back for it now!"

That was enough for Robert Dunbar, Jr. He hastily replaced the Arisaka against the wall, snatched up his Springfield, and bolted from the cave into the clear air, for the fog had drifted out to sea, or had risen high in the cove. There, not a hundred yards away, lay the silent and sinister shape of the Japanese submarine, like some deadly killer whale that had nosed up to the beach to watch Bob and Gary.

Gary braked to a halt. "Whoooeee!" he gasped. "Don't ever leave me so fast again!"

"Quiet!" said Bob. He faded back behind some rocks and studied the submarine. There was something odd about it, something that wasn't quite right. Then he realized the stern was very low in the water. She might be resting on the bottom, or perhaps had taken on enough water to lower her stern. There was an eeriness about that submarine, lying in that lonely cove, with the washing of the surf across her afterdecks, and not a soul to be seen about her.

"You don't suppose they saw us, do you?" Gary

whispered. He wet his lips. "Maybe they're hiding on the cliff or along the beach, or maybe even on board."

Bob peered through the grayness of the night. It didn't seem to be getting any darker. He looked up and realized with a start that there must be a moon above the drifting fog, giving off enough light so that objects could be dimly seen. If the fog drifted off, the island would be bathed in clear light. By the same token, the two boys from *Otter* would be fully revealed.

"We oughta get out of here," breathed Gary.

Bob wanted to leave as much as Gary did, but the thought kept reoccurring to him that perhaps that submarine was really abandoned, and if she was, there could be spare parts for her diesels still aboard — parts that *Otter* desperately needed.

"Chuck and Bennie will be looking for us," said Gary.

Bob stood up. He leaned his rifle within a crevice. "I'm going to take a closer look at that sub," he said quietly.

"I figured that was what you'd say."

"Go find Bennie and Chuck."

"And leave you? Not on your life!"

Bob turned slowly. "Look, Gary," he said, "the lives of everyone aboard *Otter* may depend on one of us taking a look at that sub. If there are Japs around, we'll need the help of Chuck and Bennie. I'll scout the sub. You go get them."

"You're leaving the easy part to me, eh?" said Gary fiercely.

Bob shook his head. "We can't get up out of this cove the way we came down into it. I think the Japs found the only way to get out of here. Through the cave and up that steep valley. Supposing you go up that way and run into some of those Japs?"

129

Gary's dirty face paled. "I never thought of that," he said.

Bob slid an arm about Gary's shoulders. "It's a job we have to do."

They padded toward the cave. Gary swallowed hard, smiled weakly, then bravely vanished into the cave.

Bob worked his way along below the cliff face, never taking his eyes from the submarine. She was streaked with rust and her outer hull was scarred and battered, although that was no indication as to how long she had been lying there. Service in Aleutian waters treated all vessels that way. He hid behind a boulder and studied the deserted-looking craft, the beach, the shore extending on either hand, and finally the dimly seen cliff face. The cove seemed as deserted as the submarine itself.

He took his waning courage into his hands and padded toward the sub, taking his pistol from its holster, and keeping his thumb on the safety. The portside of the vessel rested against a wide rock shelf that extended into the dark waters, almost like a natural dockside. Several lines trailed from the superstructure deck to lie on the rock. He holstered his Colt and pulled himself up onto the rust-streaked deck. The sea moaned and gurgled in and out of the many drain openings at the after end of the raised superstructure deck, part of which was underwater.

His feet made little noise, as he was wearing rubber-soled shoe pacs. He peeled off his parka and thrust it into an opening in the deck, then he climbed the rusted ladder to the tiny bridge of the vessel. The hatch leading into the hull was open, and it was as dark as pitch beneath the hatch. He studied it for a full five minutes, screwing his courage to the breaking point, then he let himself down onto the bridge deck and knelt by the open hatch to listen.

130

The noise of the water washing about the hull made it impossible to hear anything else. A dank, foul odor drifted up from the opening.

Bob felt for his flashlight, took one look up at the mysterious gray sky, and felt for the first rungs of the ladder with his feet. Down he went, slowly and shakily, feeling the steel of the hull close about him, as well as the foul dampness of the abandoned boat. Down rung after rung he went, until it seemed as though he'd never reach the bottom in that well of darkness, until at last his feet rested on a steel deck and he knew he was within the conning tower. The engine room would be aft, as they always were in submarines, as far as he knew. All he had to do now was to find his way to the diesels.

11

THE small yellow eye of the flashlight stabbed into the stygian gloom of the submarine as Bob Dunbar felt his way along within the unfamiliar vessel. He was now quite sure she was empty of life, although there might be bodies of her crew aboard. It wasn't likely she had had an accident at sea and had miraculously drifted into the safety of the cove. The foot and wheel marks on the beach disproved that. Whatever had happened to her had probably happened while she was entering the cove, or was well within it. A sharp-fanged rock might have seriously penetrated her pressure hull, or perhaps had destroyed her propeller, rudder, or diving fins — any one of which would have been serious enough to force her crew to abandon her.

He held his flashlight in his left hand and the pistol in his right while he inched aft in the crowded and cluttered passageway. She wasn't a large craft, perhaps hardly more than five hundred to seven hundred tons displacement, but the slow, dark journey seemed interminable to Bob, almost as though he was probing into the sunken hull of some great ship, rather than into a rather small prewar type of enemy submarine.

Dull echoes followed his steps as he went along the downward slant of the hull through the narrow passageway. There was little enough space in the bigger subs, but it seemed to Bob that a child would have a hard time finding room to move about in this boat. She was an old one. Neither the Americans nor the Japanese were using their best and latest types of naval craft in Aleutian waters.

He stopped to listen. Even his breathing sounded loud to him as he stood there feeling the icy coldness penetrating through his damp clothing. It was cold enough outside, but this was a different type of cold — an evil type of cold, malignant and foul with the concentrated mephitic odors of years of service with improper ventilation. The U.S. Navy nickname for the older type of submersible was "pigboat" and the name had been well earned.

Bob looked back into the thick darkness behind him. It was almost as though someone or something evil was watching him from that malevolent darkness, baring now and then a naked, sharp fang behind loose wet lips in anticipation of the devil's feast it would have. An icy fear swept over him, far more chilling than the actual coldness of the boat. There in the confines of that deserted enemy boat he fought the hardest mental battle of his young life, wanting to flee screaming to the deck and over the side away from the unseen horrors plaguing his teeming mind, but something else held him there, knowing he had a duty to perform upon which the lives of his comrades might depend.

A voice seemed to come from the enveloping darkness of the submarine's interior. *A man has to have time to find himself, kid. Someday the experience will come to you. It won't be a pleasant one.*

He knew that voice. It was that of his uncle Mack Dunbar. He had spoken those words on the day *Otter* had left Adak Harbor for Cape Yakok, when Bob had mentioned

133

something about Thor Andreason. At that time Bob had not been quite sure what his uncle had meant. He knew now.

The engine room watertight door was just ahead of him. It had not been dogged shut, but hung half open. Bob stepped inside and felt the icy water rise to his calves. He flicked the light about and saw the cramped confines of the compartment. It was deserted. The after end was thigh-deep in black-looking water. He waded to the diesel engine and examined it. One of the problems Jim Brannon had with the diesel engine aboard the *Otter* was with the lubricating system. Something about a broken or cracked casting in the circulating pump, and there was no spare pump available closer than Adak. Diesel engines are much alike, thought Bob, as he flashed the light foot by foot over the Japanese engine. He noticed a nameplate on it. It was an American diesel engine, probably bought in the pre-war days when thousands and thousands of tons of scrap metal were being shipped to Japan from the United States to be turned into weapons of war now being used against the United States. There had been other items sold to Japan in those days and among them had been gasoline and diesel engines, ship engines and truck engines, as well as airplane motors and many other necessary power plants without which modern wars cannot be fought.

The diesel engine in front of him looked as though it was in good shape. Jim Brannon would have to look at it. Bob poked about in the cramped room. He found tools and cased spare parts still stored there, some of them under the corroding salt water that was almost a yard deep at the after end of the compartment. Beyond the engine room was the motor room, but there was no need for Bob to explore back there. He had found what he wanted. He

134

grinned in relief. Now to get out of this gigantic steel coffin as quickly as he could and convey the good news back to the *Otter*.

He turned and flicked the light toward the forward end of the compartment and his heart seemed to fail within him. Something blocked the doorway, and even as the beam of the flashlight identified it for what it was, it started down the greasy slope of the water-covered engine room deck. It was a Japanese seaman. A fairly big man. Naked to the waist in that biting cold, wearing only a filthy breechclout about his middle and a curious-looking little cap on his head, lined with black stripes. His face was set and fierce and in his strong hands was a samurai sword. The flashlight picked out the highlights on the finely chased blade.

Bob tried to yell, but it died in his dry throat. He threw himself to one side as the blade swished over his head to clang against the metal bulkhead. He scrambled over the engine and dropped to his knees in the icy water just as the blade swung toward him again. He flicked out the flashlight and scuttled up the slope, slipping and falling as he fought for hand and foot holds, while behind him in the thick darkness he heard the harsh breathing of the man and the muttering of his voice and he realized that he was dealing with a madman.

He reached the forward end of the engine and clawed for the doorway. Metal rang like a bell against metal, inches behind him. As he pulled himself through the door something ripped at the back of his thick jacket. He swung about and kicked out as hard as he could, feeling his shoe pac sole strike flesh. An agonized grunt emerged from the Japanese. A great splashing sound came to Bob as he tried to slam the door shut and dog it, but it had jammed or

135

rusted in the hinges. He fought his way along the passage-way, feeling protuberances tear at his clothing, while his rubber-soled footgear slipped on the greasy deck plating like a squirrel in a treadmill. His breath came harshly in his throat.

His head banged into something. Even though he was half stunned he knew it was the ladder leading up into the conning tower. He stabbed his feet for the rungs as his hands clawed for the ladder sides. Halfway up the ladder a pair of powerful hands closed about his ankles. He kicked hard and viciously as he pulled himself by sheer strength into the narrow confines of the conning tower where a faint, intermittent light came down from the open hatch-way above his head. In the vague light he saw the man's head emerge from the hatchway through which the ladder protruded. He kicked out once more and started for the second ladder that led up to the tiny bridge of the sub-marine.

A hard body slammed into Bob from the rear and drove him against the side of the conning tower. He slipped down to his knees and twisted about to face his opponent. Just as he turned, the samurai blade flickered over his head and he bent low. The blade tip shattered on the unyielding bulkhead just above Bob. He drove himself to his feet, butting with his head into the hard stomach of the Japa-nese. Foul breath wheezed out from the Jap and he staggered awkwardly back to hit the opposite bulkhead. His sword dropped to the deck.

Bob shot up the second ladder like a monkey on a string and dived for the edge of the bridge, falling over it to land heavily on the rusty superstructure. He winced in pain as his knee crashed into the metal. He rolled over and over and got to his feet in a crouching position.

136

"What're you doing, Bob?" a cheerful voice said. "Practicing Abandon Ship?"

Bob stared at Gary, who was standing at the side of the conning tower, hands thrust deeply into his parka pockets, a wide grin on his dirty face. Just above Gary a head appeared and then a powerful naked arm holding a shining steel blade. The blade was drawn back for a shearing blow at the head of the unsuspecting boy. "Look out, Gary!" yelled Bob.

Gary stared at him. "You gone Aleutian-happy?" he demanded.

Then and only then did Bob remember his automatic pistol. He dragged it from its holster and snapped off the safety as he raised the heavy weapon. The sights seemed to align themselves as he squeezed the trigger and felt the pistol jerk upward in hard recoil. Smoke drifted off on the wind. The Japanese dropped the blade. It struck Gary atop the head and clattered on the deck. Seconds later the body of the Japanese hit the superstructure deck, rolled over to the edge. It bounced heavily from the rounded side of the outer hull and rolled over and over to plunge into the dark water between the side of the boat and the natural rock wharf beside it. The odd little cap floated on the water.

The echo of the shot fled wildly about the cove seeking an exit, rebounding from cliff face to cliff face, and faded away as the smoke had faded away in the wind.

Bob lowered the smoking pistol and his stomach seemed to rise and fall queasily. A moment later a sour taste came into the back of his dry throat and he retched violently as he went down on one knee. It had been so close, not only for Bob, trapped within that echoing submarine, but for Gary Lunt, who had unwittingly blundered almost into the hands of death in the shape of an obviously insane enemy.

Gary picked up the damaged sword and stared at it. It was as though he still did not believe what he had seen and heard. He ran toward Bob. " We'd better get out of here," he said. " Are there any more of them in there? "

" I didn't see any," said Bob weakly.

" I found Chuck and Bennie. They agreed to scout around to see if they could locate those Japs who disappeared inland. If those Japs heard that shot . . ." His voice trailed off.

Bob put the safety on his pistol, pulled his parka from beneath the superstructure deck, and followed Gary down the side of the hull to the rock shore. Gary snatched up the floating cap. " Man, oh man! " he crowed. " What a souvenir! This is a Jap naval officer's fatigue cap, or whatever they call it."

" I can't say I'm interested," said Bob dryly.

They ran up the deserted beach and Bob retrieved his rifle. He felt sick and weak as he followed Gary into the cave and then up the steep narrow valley. Moonlight was trying to work its way through the low-hanging clouds.

Gary whistled softly three times, then three times again. A moment later a faint whistling came to them. Twice, then twice again came the signal. Gary led the way across the wet and clinging slopes to where Chuck and Bennie lay flat behind a protruding rock dike.

Chuck glared at Gary. " Which one of you dummies fired that gun down there? "

Gary jerked a thumb at Bob. Before Chuck could speak again, Gary held out the samurai sword and the soaked cap. " Seems like there was a Jap left on the sub," he said. " Bob had to kill him or he would have killed me."

Chuck stared at the cap and the sword and then at Bob. " I'll be jiggered," he said quietly. He stood up and placed a hand on Bob's shoulder. " What happened, kid? "

Bob quietly told the three of them the whole story.

Bennie rubbed his dirty face. " You think he was left in the sub apurpose? " he asked.

Bob shook his head. " All he had on was that breechclout and the funny little cap. That sub is like a deepfreeze. He must have been hiding in there somewhere and either saw or heard me." He closed his eyes and looked away, feeling the bile rise once again in his throat.

" It ain't easy to kill a man, especially the first one," said Chuck.

" One is enough," said Bob. " Jim Brannon will have to come back and look at that diesel to see if he can find the parts he needs."

Bennie hefted his rifle. " How many men does one of those subs carry? "

Bob shrugged. " She's pretty small. What they call an RO. type, I think. I saw some pictures and drawings of Jap subs when I was in the naval hospital at Dutch. The one down there looks as if it's between five and seven hundred tons displacement. Maybe a crew of between thirty-five to forty at the very most."

" That's a few more than we have," said Chuck.

Bob looked quickly at him. " What are you thinking about? " he asked.

Chuck grounded his rifle and looked across the vague and unreal landscape, misted here and there by the creeping fog, faintly illuminated by the moonlight penetrating the thick cloud layers. " It'll take time for Jim to get the parts outa that sub," he said. " Supposing the crew comes back while he's getting the stuff out? "

" I never thought of that," said Bob.

" Get down! " snapped Bennie Dutton. He hit the

139

ground and lay still, thrusting forward his rifle.

The three of them dropped flat behind the rock dike. There was no sound other than the faint booming of the surf, and then a faint and regular sucking noise came to them. Bob raised his head a little. Not fifty yards away, hurrying across the wet and yielding tundra, was a little man wearing a rounded steel helmet beneath which could be seen a large pair of round, black spectacles. There was no mistaking his origin. He looked exactly like the libelous cartoons that were regularly appearing in American newspapers to depict the Japanese soldier.

Even as Bob stared the man turned quickly to look toward the rock dike. It was hardly possible that he did not see the four, dark hunched shapes lying there. For a long, long moment he stared toward them before he trotted toward the mouth of the shallow valley and silently disappeared.

"Supposing he spots that dead Jap?" said Gary softly.

"You said the Jap fell into the drink," said Chuck. "He won't be up for a while."

"I wonder where the rest of them are?" said Bob.

Chuck shifted a little and peered across the top of the rocks. "That's up to me and Bennie to find out. You fellows head back to *Otter* and tell 'em about the Jap sub. We'll meet you in that valley about a quarter of a mile from here. The one with the three big rock formations sticking up. Get moving!"

Gary and Bob wasted no time. They walked quickly and as silently as possible toward where *Otter* was hidden in the cove. It was too close to the cove where the sub had been abandoned to suit Bob. If Japanese were that close about, they might find *Otter*. Just before they reached the lip of the valley where they were to rendezvous later with the two Alaskan Scouts, they looked back, then as quickly hit the tundra. The little man had reappeared and this time he was carrying a rifle as he trotted past the rock dike and vanished again.

Gary Lunt chuckled.

Bob eyed his friend. " Why the laugh? "

" I was thinking about two things."

" Such as? "

Gary stood up. " First, I think that little fellow was the one who left his rifle in the cave. The one we found down there. I can imagine the reaming he got from his noncom when he was sent back for it, and the worse reaming he'll get when he gets back."

Bob grinned in appreciation. " Yeh! And the second thing? "

Gary picked up his rifle. " How'd you like to *feel* those two Alaskan Scouts back there watching you, and *you* couldn't see *them?* "

Bob nodded. The Japanese would never see Chuck and Bennie until they killed or captured him. They were like ghosts when they drifted across the soft, clinging tundra. They'd find the enemy camp or hideout and have it well scouted by the time the two boys returned from *Otter* with the men from the vessel.

" How many of them do you think there are? " said Gary quietly as they walked down into the valley and passed behind the cover of the first rock formation.

" Maybe thirty-five or forty."

It was shortly before dawn when Bob and Gary reached the cove where *Otter* lay helpless. In the shifting veils of cold fog they worked their way down the treacherous and steep slopes of tundra and rock. Sometimes they could see the vessel only to have it concealed wholly or partly by the fog that persisted in drifting over the silent island and flowing down into the hollows and over the seaside cliffs like a deadly gas of World War I vintage.

Not a light showed on the *Otter*. She seemed deserted, but both boys knew there would be men awake and at the guns both on the *Otter* and on shore. The cove and the area around it seemed deserted and far from any living human creatures other than the crew itself. But always in those islands, in peace or war, there was the uncanny feeling, experienced by those who have spent time there, that there is *something* in the fog. *Something* . . .

"Maybe they left her," whispered Gary.

"Not on your life, kid," said Bob. He felt the wet sand beneath his feet as he reached the bottom of the last slope, not over a hundred yards from *Otter*.

The two of them stood there, rifles at hip level, cocked and ready to shoot, with fog playing strange tricks with their vision. Bob had the horrible thought that maybe the Japanese had found *Otter*, had slaughtered her crew, and were on board her, waiting for the rest of the crew to return into a trap of hot lead and cold steel.

Gary Lunt voiced the thought. "Maybe the Japs took her," he hissed.

"There's only one way to find out," said Bob. "Stay here." He padded forward trying to hear above the insistent washing of the surf and the faint sighing of the wind among the rocky crags. He was cold and he was wet and his nerves were held together with string and bailing wire. He knew now that war was less of glory than it was of sheer nerve and patience for the vast majority of servicemen, and that a man had to go on no matter how tired and frightened he was.

He saw the blunt bows of the vessel, but there was no

sign of life aboard her. He had the uncanny feeling he was being watched from above. He raised his head and looked upward through the swirling mist and saw the crow's nest of the *Otter* protruding above the layers of fog. A man was in it, sighting down a rifle at him. Bob took a long chance. After all, he could always run for it. " It's me! " he called out. " Bob Dunbar! Don't shoot! " He poised on the balls of his feet, ready to sprint for cover.

For a long moment the man stood there, almost as though he was asleep or dead, and then he moved. " Come on aboard, kid," he said. It was the welcome voice of Mack Dunbar.

" Wait until I get Gary," said Bob.

" No need," said Gary from behind Bob. " I've been right behind you, Bob."

They clambered aboard and walked slowly aft to meet the skipper, who was descending the ratlines. Mack peered at them as he reached the deck. " We had almost given you boys up for lost," he said in a low voice. " Where are the others? "

" Let's get below," said Gary through chattering teeth. " All of a sudden, I remembered how nice it is below, with hot coffee and something dry to wear."

A dim light showed in the messroom. While Gary and Bob sat wrapped in dry blankets and sipped strong coffee, Bob told Mack Dunbar, Jim Brannon, and Thor Andreason of their experiences. Mike Pucci and Smitty had elected to stay on guard at the twenty millimeter gun, watch and watch until *Otter* was ready for sea again, while Jesse Easter bunked on the deck beside his fifty caliber machine gun. Baldy, the cook, was up in the crow's nest on guard, replacing the skipper.

It was Jim Brannon who finally broke the silence that

143

followed the ending of Bob's story. "I've been holding off telling you, Skipper," he said, "but I can't possibly repair our diesel. I've tried every angle I know. The lube system is stripped down to the last fitting, but unless I can get a spare pump, or a replacement casting for a circulating pump, that engine of ours is completely out of business. From what Bob here says, it might be possible to find a spare pump in that sub, or if not, I might make do with the pump on the diesel in the sub."

Mack Dunbar began to fill his pipe, eyeing each of his men from beneath his shaggy eyebrows. "How long would it take to strip off the pump on the Jap diesel?" he asked.

Jim shrugged. "An hour at the least if I have help." He looked at Mack, but not at Thor, and all of them, including Thor, knew what he was thinking. Down inside that icy tomb of a sub and working knee-deep in freezing seawater, one could be trapped by fierce Japanese seamen and Marines. But he needed Thor's help.

Thor Andreason raised his head. "I'll go," he said quietly. He looked at Bob. "If the kid here can go alone down into that sub to see if the pump could be used on *Otter's* engine, and kill a crazed Jap in the process, I guess there isn't any question of *me* holding back."

Mack lighted his pipe. "No one can hold back," he said. "Win or lose, we have to make the last cast of the dice. There'll be no going back once we start this thing."

"When do we start?" asked Jim.

Mack drew in on his pipe and blew a perfect smoke ring toward the dim lamp. "No time like the present," he said. "The fog might hold on. I've always hated fog, but this day we'll need it as we never needed it before. We need that pump. Therefore we go and get it. One more thing: those Japs are up to no good on this island." He stood up

144

and looked down at them. "None of you knew about this, but within the next week or so, according to what I have heard, American troops will land upon and occupy this island. As far as they know, it's empty of Jap troops. Maybe we'll have to make *sure* it is. You follow me, lads?"

None of them answered. Mack Dunbar's words had been etched into their minds. *No one can hold back. Win or lose, we have to make the last cast of the dice. There'll be no going back once we start this thing.*

The lamplight raised the highlights on the naked steel of the samurai blade that the boys had brought from the Japanese submarine and on the filthy, salt-stained cap of the man Bob had killed to save Gary's life. There were probably many more of those keen blades worn at the sides of tough Japanese who were ashore on Amchitka that day. They would also be well armed with Arisaka rifles, Nambu automatic pistols, long bayonets, and a variety of automatic weapons.

"Landing party ashore," said Mack Dunbar quietly. "All hands! Jump and make it so, boys!"

12

T<small>HE</small> *Otter* would have to be temporarily abandoned. The decision had been Mack Dunbar's. Not a man could be spared to guard her. The life of the vessel, and quite possibly that of her crew, depended on a simple, commonplace circulating pump for a disabled diesel engine. The thought was almost ridiculous except for the fact that it was indeed deadly important. The lives of men and of ships depend sometimes on simple, commonplace things. For want of a nail the battle was lost.

Each man carried several days' hard rations as well as his weapons and one blanket. The twenty millimeter gun had been disabled by the removal of vital parts, and then the weapon had been hidden beneath a tarp covered by the long and matted grass of the tundra. The barrel of the fifty caliber machine gun had been removed and hidden ashore. There was nothing else that could be done. No man looked back as Bob Dunbar, clad in fresh dry clothing, led the way up the cliff face followed by as motley an assortment of potential fighting men as history might ever record.

Bob could not help thinking of Dunbar's Irregulars, as Gary had solemnly dubbed them, as he led the way along the cliff edge toward the valley to rendezvous with Chuck MacIver and Bennie Dutton. Led by an aging ex-chief petty officer of World War I, Dunbar's Irregulars consisted of two semi-outcast twenty millimeter gunners from the Navy, *without* their gun; a lost soul from the Army, "I'm whut they call a casual" Easter; a fifty caliber machine gunner also without his gun; an aging diesel engineer from the Bering Sea Patrol; a maimed and neurotic veteran of Pearl Harbor; two boys not yet eighteen; and two Alaskan Scouts, the last named probably the best and most efficient fighting men of the lot.

Somewhere within the shrouding fog were an unknown number of trained Japanese fighting men from the abandoned submarine, quite likely armed to the teeth, and ready to fight to the last man as was their fierce feudal custom. No matter what else anyone thought of the Japanese, no one had ever questioned their devotion to duty and their courage.

It was Bob Dunbar who flitted alone into the foggy valley that early morning and located the two Scouts. He went back and led up the rest of the "landing" party. They stood around in a solemn circle, leaning on their rifles, listening to Chuck MacIver's urgent whispering voice as he briefed them in on what he and Bennie had discovered.

"There are about thirty-five or forty of them, as Bob estimated," said Chuck. "Most of them are sailors, as far as we can guess, but they got some big, tough-looking characters in what look like Army uniforms, only with a Navy-looking insignia. Bennie thinks the same as I do. They're Jap Marines, and we don't have to tell you how tough those boys are. They're handpicked, like most Marines. Those wheel tracks we saw are from a couple of carts carrying heavy machine guns. They also have quite a few light machine guns. Quite a few for such a small party. They've holed up in a narrow valley not too far from Constantine Harbor and they seem to have plenty of stores. Enough to keep 'em alive for a couple of weeks at least. While we were scouting them, one of their scouting parties came back from the harbor. Beats us what they are doing here, unless they're waiting to be picked up."

Bob looked at his uncle and remembered the information he had given them about a possible landing of American troops on the island within a week or so.

Mack Dunbar shoved back his parka hood. "We don't know why they came here," he said quietly, "but we know what they *can* do. I already told the rest of the boys that our forces may land here in a week or so. That's the scuttlebutt, anyway, and I think it's true. A handful of Japs can't stop our boys from landing, and they wouldn't try. Can you imagine what they *can* do, though, if they let our forces scatter all around that harbor, setting up guns, building an airfield, and so on?"

Jesse Easter shifted his feet and looked uncomprehendingly at Mack Dunbar. "What do you mean, sir?" he said.

"They'd be like rangers or commandos. Hit and run. Sneak up on unguarded tents or lone sentries and cut throats under cover of the fog, or a heavy snowstorm. Sabotage planes, tractors, boats, trucks, and anything else they can get to. They can hit and run, scatter and hide, and it would take a division to find them in these coves and valleys under cover of the fog and rain. They could establish a base for more and more Jap infiltrators. We've hardly enough troops available to stop them, and we badly need this island for an advance base to clean out Kiska by bombing raids. You lads get the picture?"

"We need that circulating pump, anyway," said Jim

Brannon. "If the Japs get in our way, maybe we can do two jobs instead of one."

Mack nodded. "Chuck, you and Bennie scout ahead toward the valley that leads into the cave. Let us know if the way is clear. The rest of us will wait up on the cliff overlooking the cove. I want to get the lay of the land."

Chuck and Bennie moved out, vanishing quickly into the fog. Bob and Gary led the others toward the cliff, feeling their way cautiously along, knowing it would be too easy to step into nothingness in that fog. They found the place where they had descended the dangerous cliff face down to the cove. The cove was thick with clammy fog. The submarine was an indistinct shape beneath it, and if Bob hadn't known it was surely there, he would have doubted that it really existed.

Now and then it became lighter over the island, and once they could have sworn they heard the distant droning of an airplane motor over the fog. They caught occasional glimpses of the sea through openings in the fog. It was Jesse Easter who saw something out there. The Arkansas boy had eyes like a hawk. "Looks like a low-lying ship of some kind," he drawled. Every man looked out to sea, trying to pierce the shifting, swirling veils of fog.

Mack Dunbar uncased his binoculars and adjusted them. For a long time he said nothing. When he lowered the glasses he handed them to Mike Pucci. "See what you think," he said.

Mike studied the distant, almost invisible object. He too lowered the glasses. "Sub," he said quietly.

"One of ours?" asked Gary eagerly.

Mike shook his head. He looked at Mack Dunbar. "It's a big one," he said. "I-Class probably. I saw a picture of one of them at Pearl Harbor. Maybe two thousand tons.

149

Carries a big deck gun about five inch as far as I can recollect."

"Carries something else too," said Smitty. "A catapult reconnaissance plane, and triple twenty-five millimeter A.A. guns aft of the periscopes."

"How big a crew?" said Mack.

Mike shrugged. "Figuring from the size of *our* subs, I'd say as many as seventy-five to ninety men. They can crowd in quite a few Army men or Marines as well."

"Happy days," said Smitty. "She ain't out there hunting sea otters. You don't suppose she's hunting for the one down below us, do you, Skipper?"

Mack hefted the submachine gun he was carrying. "No use kidding ourselves, lads. That's probably just what she *is* doing out there."

"Salt, pepper, and gravel in the grease," said Jesse mournfully.

A soft whistle came to them. They all dropped to the spongy tundra and shoved their weapons forward. The whistle came twice more and then Chuck MacIver emerged through the fog. He grounded his mottled service rifle. "The game is off," he said soberly. "We spotted half a dozen Japs prowling about the mouth of the valley. None of them are down in the cave, but you'd never get past them."

"Then we can go behind them," said Mack. He looked around at Bob. "Kid, you and Gary got down there from here, didn't you?"

Bob nodded. "By sheer luck more than brains, Skipper."

Mack looked at Jim. "Can you make it, Jim?"

Jim rubbed his bristly jaws. "No choice," he said.

It was Bob who again led the way, feeling along the face of that fog-shrouded cliff for the second time. Above him was Gary Lunt and above Gary was Jim Brannon. They were to signal to the others when they reached the bottom. Thor Andreason was then to try it alone, a man with but one hand of flesh and blood. Bob had wanted to help him, but Thor had refused, saying, " If I fall, I won't want to take anyone with me." There had been no arguing with him. His mind had been thoroughly made up.

Bob reached the beach and waited for the others. He could hear Jim's harsh and erratic breathing, sounding too loud to Bob, although he knew the beating of the surf against the beach and the rocks would effectively drown it out. Gary dropped to the sand. He shook his head. " Next time I'll take the bus," he said weakly.

Jim finally made the bottom. He rested his head against the cliff face and his body shook with his labored breathing. He turned and looked at the boys. " Another fifty feet of that and I wouldn't have had to climb down. I would have dropped like a stone."

Bob walked back and whistled softly three times. The cliff face was wreathed in fog, and they had no way of knowing Thor was on his way down until three stones landed among them, one of them neatly clobbering Gary atop his bare head. The three of them stood well back from the cliff with the surf washing almost about their feet, staring up into the gray milkiness, half expecting to see Thor hurtling down with a thin screaming until he hit the studded rocks below. Minute after minute ticked past. A piece of rock clattered against the cliff face and struck the sand with a soft thudding sound. Five minutes ticked past. A rifle struck the sand butt first, followed by a heavy cartridge belt and holstered pistol.

" He's hung up for sure! " breathed Jim Brannon. " We should have made him stay up there! "

Dirt and grass drifted down through the fog. Bob fanned impatiently at the fog as though to clear the way for his vision. Then he saw a dark shape forty feet up on the cliff face. It was Thor all right, hanging there, staring down through the treacherous fog with set white face. Bob's heart went out to him. He peeled off parka and cartridge belt, leaned his rifle against a rock, and ran forward to the base of the cliff, scaling it as swiftly as he could, until he was beside Thor. He looked into the taut face of the man, dewed with clammy sweat. He smiled. " I'll show you the way, Thor," he said.

Foot by foot Bob guided the maimed veteran down the cliff, expecting at any second to be struck by the man's body as it fell from the cliff face and carried them both to death below. Only when Bob felt his feet on the beach and saw Thor standing beside him did he resume normal breathing. " You've got more than your share of nerve, kid," said Thor.

" Listen to *him*," said Gary, " talking about nerve."

Jim came to them. " This is all very nice," he said, " but it isn't getting that pump out of the sub. Come on! "

Gary and Bob led the way past the dark cave mouth. Gary dropped behind a rock, thrusting his rifle across it to cover the cave mouth while Bob led the others to that rusting hulk lying on the bottom of the lonely cove. He waited until he saw Jim vanish inside the conning tower, followed by Thor, and then he went back to Gary. He crouched beside him. " Speaking of nerve," he said quietly, " nothing, but absolutely nothing, could ever get me inside that steel coffin again! "

" Wouldn't bother *me*," said Gary stoutly.

Bob raised his head. " Hey," he said. " Jim left his tools on the beach. Go get 'em, Gary, and bring 'em down to the boys in the engine room." He grinned as he saw the look on his friend's face. " Forget it. They took the tools along with 'em."

" Yeh," said Gary with a wan smile, " I knew it alla time."

As much as Bob watched the dark mouth of the cave, half expecting to see a file of Japanese sailors or Marines pop out of it, he could not help looking back to sea every few minutes, although his vision was blocked by the thick fog. Somewhere offshore, maybe even poking in at dead slow speed toward the land, might be that big Japanese sub looking for its smaller sister. Maybe the Japanese ashore had radioed to Kiska for help. Maybe the big I-Class boat had come for them and knew where they had abandoned the smaller sub. That's all that was needed. As Jesse Easter had said, " Salt, pepper, and gravel in the grease."

How long would it take for Jim and Thor to rip that circulating pump from the Japanese submarine? The sands of time were running slowly, much too slowly.

Up on the cliff overlooking the narrow valley were the rest of the *Otter*'s crew, watching and waiting for any attempt of the shore Japanese to enter that cave. If they started to shoot, the sound might carry far enough to sea for the crew of the I-Class boat to hear it.

" And we were worried we weren't going to get into the war," whispered Gary.

Gary shifted. " Maybe they ran into more of them boys like the one you scuppered," he said. " Might be a wild brawl going on in there right now and we can't see or hear a thing."

" Will you shut up! " snapped Bob.

Gary flushed. " Well," he said, " I was only thinking.

153

Fellow can't even express an opinion anymore."

"Some opinion." Bob glanced at his watch. Somehow an hour had drifted past. "An hour at least if I have help," Jim had said when asked how long it would take to get the pump off the engine. The thought came to Bob that maybe Thor Andreason had cracked again, in that partly flooded engine room, and that maybe Jim was fighting for his life against the crazed veteran as Bob had fought for his own life against the crazed Japanese who had somehow been left, or had stayed hidden aboard the sub when his comrades had left. He stood up and leaned his rifle against the rocks. He took out his Colt and loaded it, the metallic action of the slide sounding inordinately loud.

Gary stared at him. "What's up?"

"I'll have to go after them," said Bob.

"In there?"

"*They're* in there, aren't they?" demanded Bob fiercely.

"Wait," said Gary. He turned and looked at the indistinct mouth of the cave, dimly seen through the thickening fog. Bob stared at it as well. Something was warning them — an uncanny sixth sense. The fog seemed to be enveloping the whole island, seeping into valleys and hollows, swirling down into the coves and the beaches, thickening and thickening, hiding everything from view.

Gary wet his lips and glanced quickly at Bob. "You feel it too?" he whispered.

Bob nodded. "Get down," he said. "Low!"

Something was moving within the mouth of the cave, and a moment later a man appeared, wearing a rounded helmet and carrying a rifle. Even at that distance, through the concealing fog, there was something alien about the man. His stance, his movements, his clothing, all bespoke his race. He was Japanese.

154

"How did he get past our men?" whispered Gary.

"The fog concealed him," said Bob softly. "I wonder how many more of them it concealed."

"Look!" said Gary.

Several more helmeted Japanese appeared, moving softly on the black sand, peering toward the abandoned submarine. There was no time to warn Jim and Thor. They'd have to shoot to hold those men away from the submarine. Two boys against at least a squad of Japanese Marines, for these men were surely not sailors. More of them appeared out of the cave as though conjured up by some Oriental genie.

Bob turned over the safety of his rifle. He didn't want to shoot. As far as he knew, the Japanese did not know there were Americans on Amchitka. If they did find out, they'd track down the little crew of the *Otter* and slaughter them. They had the men and weapons with which to do so.

"Look!" said Gary. He pointed toward the submarine.

A man's head appeared above the bridge, looking toward Bob and Gary. It was Jim Brannon. Bob took a long chance. He stood up, hoping the fog would conceal him from the enemy, and waved violently at Jim, then pointed toward the beach. Jim stared for a moment, looking toward the beach. It was hardly possible to distinguish the Japanese, but fog plays weird tricks, and one of them is to carry voices for great distances. Some of the men were talking and the sound carried to Jim. He disappeared down behind the bridge like a bristle-chinned jack-in-the-box.

Feet churned through the loose sand. The voices came closer. Equipment rattled. Bob sank down behind Gary. They were close up against the northern cliff face, with thirty feet of beach between them and the natural rock

155

wharf against which lay the submarine. The rock dike behind which they were concealed was hardly three feet high. If one of those Marines happened to look over it, it would be all up for Gary, Bob, and maybe the rest of the *Otter*'s crew.

Bob pressed his face close to the hard cold rock and his hands tightened on the stock of his rifle. Any second now he and Gary might have to face a stand-up fight against trained Marines, experts at infighting, merciless combat killers.

Nothing moved on Gary except his eyes, wide in his head. He too was coiled like a spring, ready to jump up and start shooting, for he knew as well as Bob did that there would be no quarter in this type of fighting. Actually civilians had no right to fight them, and the penalty was simple enough if they were known to be civilians. They might capture servicemen instead of killing them, but for civilians to resist them the penalty was death. It had been different at Pearl Harbor, of course, for many American civilians, men, women, and children, had died during the sneak attack.

Bob turned his eyes and his stomach turned as well, for he could see the helmeted head of one of the Japanese above his shoulders. He was talking rapidly to one who was unseen. If he so much as turned his head a quarter of the way around, he could not fail to see the two boys lying there.

More voices came out of the fog. Feet grated on mingled sand and rock. A rifle was leaned against the rock dike, so close that Bob could see the shielded front sight and the end of the cleaning rod. He could touch it with little effort if he wanted to.

There was nothing to do but lie there and sweat it out.

There were at least a dozen of them within spitting distance of Bob and Gary, from the sound of the voices, at least, and perhaps many more of them were beyond earshot. Bob dared turn his head. He could see past the end of the dike to the stern of the rusting submarine with the afterpart below the surging waters. There was something else there too, lying on a sea-washed rock shelf, half hidden by kelp. He closed his eyes and felt green bile rise in the back of his throat, and he knew he was going to be deathly sick at any instant. The body of the man he had killed had been washed up astern of the submarine. If the others saw it, they also could see the bullet hole in the dead man's head. Perhaps they were looking for him. They wouldn't have to look very hard now.

Feet thudded on the metal of the submarine's outer hull and a Japanese called out to another. Metal struck metal. Then as Bob opened his eyes again he saw several of the Japanese standing as far astern as they could on the hull without getting their feet wet, looking down into the water, talking animatedly. All they had to do was look forty-five degrees to their right and they'd hardly miss seeing the body.

There was no sound from the submarine other than the voices of the Japanese. Perhaps Jim and Thor had already been captured, perhaps killed in the icy wet interior of the submarine, or were perhaps hiding as best they could from the intruders.

Minutes drifted past with agonizing slowness. Then the rifle that was leaning against the dike was picked up. A sharp command was given. The men disappeared from the stern of the submarine. Feet slogged through the thick wet sand. Equipment rattled. Voices faded away.

Bob gathered his courage and looked around the end

of the dike. He could see the last files of the squad as they slogged toward the cave mouth. In a few minutes they had disappeared inside the cave and it was quiet again except for the distant booming of the surf beyond the cove and the gurgling of the tide as it washed back and forth alongside the abandoned submarine.

Bob slowly stood up with his rifle at the ready. The beach was deserted. He could see the mingled tracks of the Japanese. " Stay here," he said to Gary. He ran toward the submarine, glancing toward the corpse of the dead Japanese as he did so. The body was gone, washed back into the concealing sea once again. Bob shuddered. He clambered aboard the submarine and up the side of the conning tower to peer into the bridge. The hatch was still open. " Jim! " he called.

" Coming, kid," said the muffled voice from the control room. " They gone? "

" I wouldn't be here if they hadn't gone."

" Figures."

Jim appeared, carrying the circulating pump. He worked his way up the ladder and deposited the heavy pump on the bridge. Bob helped him get the pump down to the deck and then across to where Gary was waiting. Bob looked back at the sub. Thor's blond thatch showed above the bridge. " I'll give him a hand," said Bob. He hurried back to help Thor.

Thor passed down a sack of parts and tools. " That was a close one," he said. His face was white and set. " We heard them talking in the control room. We waded back into the motor room and closed the door, standing up to our waists in water. They came into the engine room and we thought it was all up. We had taken the pump off and when we heard them we dropped it under the water. We didn't want them to see it lying atop the engine. They tried the motor room door, but two scared Americans totaling about three hundred and fifty pounds were leaning up against it. Then they left. We don't know what they were looking for."

Thor picked up the sack. " Let's get out of here! "

" Wait," said Bob. A small wooden box was lying just behind the conning tower. He picked it up and opened it. Neat rows of flares were in it. He had not seen it on the deck before the Japanese had appeared in the cove. " This is why they came here," added Bob. He looked aft. From the rear of the submarine one could get a narrow view of the sea through the drifting fog. " They wanted to signal to that I-Boat out there."

Jim Brannon hurried toward them. " Let's go! " he snapped.

Bob showed him the flares. " They intended to signal out to sea," he said. " The fog was too thick."

Jim grinned. " Take 'em along," he said. " Maybe we can do a little tricky signaling ourselves."

Bob eyed the box. " Wait! " he said. He placed the box where he had found it and then climbed back onto the bridge. He let himself down into the conning tower despite the horrible chilly feeling he always got around that accursed vessel. He saw a locker and opened it. By sheer luck there were several boxes exactly like the one he had found on deck. Racked behind them was an awkward-looking flare pistol. He took it from the rack and carried box and pistol back to the outer deck. Quickly he studied the flares. They had been tipped with coloring obviously to indicate the color of the exploding flare. They were identical in each box. He followed the others ashore with a vague plan feeling its way into his mind.

Chuck MacIver appeared at the mouth of the cave as they slogged along the beach. " Hump it! " he snapped. " The Japs have pulled out, heading back to their camp! No time to waste! "

" Who was thinking of wasting time? " said Gary dryly.

They hurried into the cave, knowing their tracks would be lost among those of the enemy, and worked their way up the greasy floor of the valley. The fog was like a gray pall as they reached the mouth of the valley and felt their way toward the others. Three soft whistles were answered by as many. In a matter of minutes the little party was moving as quickly as possible through the clinging fog with the precious circulating pump in the midst of them, guarded as though it was the Hope diamond.

13

A STRANGLING tension settled about the lonely cove and the beached *Otter*. The fog still held sway, but there was no telling when it would lift or drift away on the wind. There was little or no wind, but that didn't mean a thing. Wind can rise swiftly and disastrously in the Aleutians and if it did, within the next twenty-four hours it would sweep away the fog with an invisible broom, revealing *Otter* where she lay helplessly, and allowing the prowling I-Boat to come closer to the treacherous coast. Meanwhile there were the Japanese on Amchitka, enough of them to attack and capture *Otter* and her crew.

With the fog had come a penetrating cold that passed right through the thickest clothing with ease. The hell of the Vikings was thought to be a cold and icy place of darkness as compared to the better-known hell of burning heat and leaping flames. Much can be said for both theories as ideals of the worst punishment man can suffer. The *Otter*'s crew was experiencing the cold hell.

Sleep had to be snatched whenever possible. Every man was dead weary, but most of them were unable to rest. Guard had to be stood while Thor and Jim replaced the lubricating pump on the balky diesel. It was morale-shaking to stand guard in that creeping fog and piercing cold, staring into the drifting opaqueness with red-rimmed eyes, watching and waiting, listening to every sound that might carry above the incessant drumming of the seas on that forgotten coast. Time became a dawdling sluggard.

Bob Dunbar huddled in the pit that Chuck MacIver and Bennie Dutton had dug at the top of the trail that led slantwise down the treacherous cliff to the beach near *Otter*. Bob kept peering through the fog, but Chuck slept like a child, huddled in blankets at the bottom of the pit. Somewhere out in the fog was Bennie Dutton, backed up by, of all people, sleepy Jesse Easter upon whom cold acted like an extreme allergy. There had been no choice in the matter. It was as Mack Dunbar had said, " No one can hold back."

A soft whistle sounded down on the trail. A pause. Then two whistles. A pause and two more. Bob turned to see Gary poke his head up where the trail reached the cliff brink. Gary slid into the pit and grinned. " They got the pump on," he said. " They sent me up to tell you they have to test run the engine. Can't take any chances of it failing when we try to get offshore."

Bob winced. " This fog will carry the sound of that engine for a mile," he said.

" You got any better ideas? "

Bob shook his head. He woke up Chuck, much as he hated to do so, and told him the news.

Chuck rubbed the sleep from his eyes. " Can't be helped," he said. " Bennie come back yet? "

" No."

Chuck peered over the edge of the pit. " Shoulda been back by now."

Bob raised his head. Something was moving out in the fog. A moment later the agreed-upon whistle signal came through the mist. A shambling figure moved toward them and the tired face of Jesse Easter peered at them from beneath the parka hood. "Man," he said. "We got trouble."

Chuck stood up quickly. "What do you mean? Where's Bennie?"

"Out theah watching them."

"Them? Who?" demanded Chuck.

Jesse coughed. "Them Japs. 'Bout eight or ten of 'em. They been prowlin' along the headland lookin' out to sea. Bennie says they're looking for that big sub out theah."

Chuck grabbed him by the parka front. "How close are they?"

"Quarter of a mile, maybe."

Chuck's face blanched. He turned quickly. "Get down there and tell 'em not to start that engine, Gary!"

Gary vanished down the greasy trail. Chuck picked up his rifle and checked it. At that instant the coughing roar of the diesel engine came up through the fog and echoed along the cliff.

Bob's heart plunged into his belly. He stared at Chuck. "They'll surely hear that," he said.

Chuck nodded. He climbed out of the pit. "They're out on the headland," he said quietly. "Sure, they'll hear it, but the rest of their party won't. *They* won't know about it unless the boys on the headland get back to tell 'em."

The engine was coughing erratically. It would take five to ten minutes for Gary to reach *Otter* and have them stop the engine. Time enough for those Japanese to hear it and spot where it came from. If they got back to the rest of the party, or somehow managed to signal the

I-Boat out at sea, it would be all over for *Otter* and her crew.

Chuck looked at his two companions. "We can't let Bennie face them all alone," he said. "We can't let 'em get back to their buddies. You follow me?"

Jesse nodded dumbly. Bob felt a more penetrating cold creep into his already chilled body. "If we start shooting, the rest of their boys might hear it," he said.

Chuck reached behind his back and drew out his issue bayonet. "I've always used this to poke up the fire or make toast," he said grimly. "Never thought I'd have to use it for what it was intended." He slid the ring over the muzzle and the catch snapped crisply on the bayonet stud at the fore end of the stock. Without another word he turned and padded off into the mist with the bayonet outthrust, as though it too was feeling its way along.

Jesse looked at Bob. "Well?"

Bob climbed out of the pit. "You said there were eight or ten of them, didn't you?" He felt for the clumsy bayonet that Mack Dunbar had insisted they all carry with them. He placed it on the rifle and walked after Chuck, who had almost vanished in the fog. A moment later he heard Jesse's squelching footsteps behind him and turned to see the Arkansan fitting his bayonet to his rifle. Bob felt sorry for him. Jesse moved slowly enough as it was, but in a bayonet fight, where speed and skill were everything, where one kills or is killed, men such as Jesse had little chance to survive. *Or unskilled civilian boys.* The latter thought pierced Bob's mind like the cold steel of a Jap bayonet. As he walked on, he heard the diesel engine splutter and then stop.

Bennie Dutton was waiting for them, lying at the reverse crest of a low ridge that extended almost completely

164

across the narrow headland. He held up a warning hand. The others dropped beside him. Bennie turned to look at Chuck. "Eight of them," he whispered. "Some sailors and some Marines. One of them was carrying a box like Bob found on the deck of the submarine and one of them goofy-looking flare pistols. Who was the idiot that started that motor?"

"Couldn't be helped," said Chuck.

"No? Look!"

They all peered through the shaggy grass that thatched the ridge. Vague figures could be seen through the shifting fog. They were standing at the edge of the headland, looking down toward the unseen cove where *Otter* lay helpless. If the fog lifted . . .

"Maybe they think it's their buddies out on that I-Boat," said Jesse hopefully in a very small voice.

Chuck shook his head. "We can't take that chance."

Bennie unbuckled his cartridge belt, peeled off his parka and jacket, and unsheathed his long-bladed knife. His rather flat face was impassive as he looked at Chuck. "I can't use one of them pig stickers," he said. "I'll try to get around behind them and pick one or two of them off to make the odds a little better."

Chuck nodded. "Try to pick *all* of 'em off, pal," he said.

"I ain't greedy. Just remember one thing: a breed Aleut might look just a little like one of them Japs in this fog."

"No chance," said Chuck. "None of them could possibly be as ugly as you."

Bennie grinned. "I knew you'd have something nice to say." Then he was gone, as silently as the drifting fog.

Chuck looked at his two companions and who could blame him if his heart failed a little? A lanky, easygoing Arkansas hillbilly who only made a semblance of speed

165

at any time, and a dirty-faced kid who had more nerve than skill. "We can't shoot," he said. "When they get wise to Bennie that's the tip-off for us. We've got to hit 'em and hit 'em hard. Get one of them right away before they know we're around. Then it's every man for himself. If they start shooting, then we can shoot, *but not before they do!*"

They lay flat on the cold tundra, bayoneted rifles in their hands, waiting for the "tip-off," as Chuck had called it. Then Bob saw a dim figure rise and disappear, rise and vanish again, not far from one of the Japanese who stood farthest out on the headland with a high hummock between him and his comrades. It happened so quickly it surprised even Bob, who was watching intently. The dim figure raced toward the unsuspecting man. The Aleut slid a big dirty hand around from behind to clamp over the man's mouth and an instant later the knife blade sank deeply through parka and flesh. The Japanese was rolled into a hollow and Bennie worked his way like a phantom around the hummock to where a second Japanese was sitting on a rock peering down into the milky fog. The rest of the party was standing in a group closer to where Chuck, Jesse, and Bob were hidden, not fifty yards away from them. Once again the knife flashed and the body was dragged behind the hummock, but this time a short, sharp cry came from the Japanese.

The six Japanese looked toward the hummock. One of them called out, then quickly unslung his bayoneted rifle and walked toward the hummock. Bennie faded around the hummock, within sight of the Americans, but still hidden from the others. He looked back toward the ridge and the three waiting there caught his message. He might be able to kill his third man, but he'd never be able to do it

166

quietly. The game was almost up as far as Bennie was concerned.

"Now!" said Chuck MacIver. Without another word he had risen to his feet and was racing across the spongy tundra toward the five Japanese who were still looking toward the hummock. There was no choice for Jesse and Bob. They rose to their feet and plunged after the Alaskan Scout.

Bennie appeared from behind the hummock in a life-and-death battle with the Japanese. The rest of the Japanese shouted and began to run toward them. One of them suddenly stopped and turned, and as he did so, Chuck MacIver was in on him, driving the bayonet in low and hard. Before the surprised man knew what had happened he was dead, but in that instant he had managed to shriek loudly.

The four Japanese turned and stared at the three Americans. Rifles swung down and the steel of the bayonets shone dully as they charged toward Chuck MacIver. He met the first of them bayonet to bayonet in a crisp, nerve-tingling jarring of tempered steel. The Marine was too skilled for Chuck. He leaped back and swung the butt of the rifle around in a hard, smashing stroke that caught the Scout alongside his head, driving him to the ground on one knee.

There was no time for Bob Dunbar to stand as a spectator, for a burly Marine was charging down on him, face set and hard, steel tip reaching out for Bob's shrinking Yankee flesh. He thrust out his rifle and it was parried expertly. He jumped to one side and tried a short thrust only to have it parried with a jarring of his rifle and his arms. His feet sank into the soft tundra and he felt unutterably weary as he kept his eyes on those of his enemy

167

as he had been taught in a half hour lesson by Chuck MacIver. The Marine moved in, always on the offense, thrusting and slashing like a butcher at his block, and the words of Chuck MacIver came back to Bob an instant before he expected the killing thrust. *The bayonet fighter must always attack; must always be on the offensive. He kills or is killed.*

A swift and totally unexpected butt stroke struck Bob cruelly on the shoulder and drove him to the ground and the man poised his long bayonet for the killing thrust, as though savoring the act.

"*Yaaaiiih!*" The sharp-pitched yell came from behind the Marine. Startled, he turned about to meet a bayonet that slammed up to the guard in his thick chest and was withdrawn an instant later while Jesse L. Easter leaped over the dead man and raced toward the Japanese who was struggling with Chuck on the spongy ground. A butt stroke laid him low. A quick in and out thrust of the red blade kept him there. "*Yaaaiiih! Yaaaiiih!*" screamed the aroused Arkansan. He plunged toward two more of the Marines.

Bennie Dutton stood over his dead opponent watching Jesse. Chuck MacIver was on his knees staring at Jesse while Bob Dunbar was running forward to help the Arkansan.

The first of the two Japanese met Jesse head on and he was a skilled bayonet fighter. Thrust, parry, slash, jab, thrust, parry, and slash was his routine, but Jesse bored in like an auger getting a bite in soft wood. He parried each thrust and drove in hard and fast, driving the screaming man back until a butt stroke knocked him galley west and a jab finished him off.

"*Yaaaiiih!*" screamed Jesse. He turned and ran toward

168

the last of the Japanese. It was too much for that son of Nippon. Maybe it was Jesse's killing skill. Maybe it was the fact that the seaman was the last of his party. To Bob Dunbar it seemed as though it was the high-pitched yelling that came from Jesse's diaphragm. It sounded like nothing human. The Japanese threw down his rifle and ran toward the cliff brink. He did not hesitate a second as he leaped out into foggy space, legs churning as he vanished from sight, leaving a thin scream hanging in the cold air.

Bob helped Chuck MacIver to his feet. He dabbled at a bloody welt on his temple. " I never seen the like. Jesse, of all people," Chuck said.

Bennie came toward them. "That yelling of his scairt even me," he said. "What was it, Jesse?"

Jesse shambled back toward them, trailing his deadly rifle and bayonet. "Rebel yell," he said quietly. " Ol' Grandpa Suggs, he was my mother's pappy, taught me it. He was with the ol' Third Arkansas during the Wah Between the States. Part of Hood's original brigade, they was. 'Hood's Texans,' they called 'em. Only Arkansas regiment in the brigade was the ol' Third Arkansas."

"Yeh," said Chuck dryly. "It was probably all they needed to fight alongside them wild-eyed Texans. Where'd you ever learn to bayonet fight like that?"

Jesse grinned. "Flunked basic trainin' twice," he said " Never could get the hang of it. All of a sudden I saw Robert here havin' a little trouble, and ol' Chuck wasn't in a very good position, so I figgered I might do something about it. Got to say one thing for it, fellas."

"Yeh?" said Bob wonderingly. "What?"

Jesse grinned again. "I'm warmed up for the first time since I hit this icebox of an island."

"That's enough for me," said Bennie. "Let's get rid of those bodies. Over the cliff with 'em. I'll scout back down the headland to make sure none of the others are around." He got his parka and rifle and disappeared into the fog.

It was a dirty, gruesome business, but it had to be done. When the three of them had finished they found another of those little wooden boxes, and in it were but three flares. Two whites and a red. Bob took them along. "The signal must be some combination of these colors. But what?"

"Whut do we care?" said Jesse mournfully. "I'm cold." He was back in character again.

They met Bennie at the base of the headland. He shook his head. "Not a sight of them," he said.

Chuck leaned wearily on his rifle. "Maybe we can get away from this island now," he said.

They walked wearily back to the trail. Bennie and Chuck stayed on guard, while Bob and Jesse worked their way down the slippery trail to the beach, made their signal to the *Otter*, and went aboard. Mack Dunbar was pacing the little bridge. He gripped the railing and looked down at Bob. "You all right, kid? Jesse? Where are the others?"

"Everyone is fine," said Bob.

"Where are the Japs?"

Bob made an expressive gesture, drawing his hand quickly across his throat. Actually he didn't feel very bloodthirsty.

"*All* of them?" said Mack incredulously.

"All of them we could find, suh," said Jesse. "Man, I'm cold."

Mack came down to the well deck and gripped Bob about the shoulders. "Tell me," he said.

Bob told him the short, but violent story. "How soon can we get out of here?" he asked with a slight break in his voice. He knew he couldn't last much longer. It had been a long, long time since they had left Adak.

"Jim says the pump works fine. We can leave as soon as the tide comes in full. In about an hour and a half."

"Whut about that Jap sub out theah, suh?" said Jesse.

"Maybe it's gone," said Mack.

Bob held out the flare box. "They were trying to signal again, Skipper. I'll swear it's still out there."

Mack nodded. "Maybe it was wishful thinking. Send Gary up to tell one of the Alaskan Scouts to come down and give us a hand. One of them will have to stick it out up there until we're ready to leave. Meanwhile, we've got to get ready for sea."

"In this fog?" said Bob.

"It'll make it difficult for us to be seen. On the other hand, it won't make it easy to get out of here. It's difficult enough when it's clear. We're trapped if we stay, and maybe we're trapped if we leave."

The tide was creeping in, almost as though it too was feeling its way in through the clinging fog. It gurgled and washed in and out of the crevices of the cove. Slowly, almost painfully, *Otter* began to raise herself from her tilted position until only her forefoot was still embedded in the bottom sand, and only her anchors held her fast to the inhospitable shore. The crew sweated the heavy disassembled twenty millimeter gun down the rugged slopes to the soft sand of the beach and stopped for a breather. It was then that Bennie Dutton, who had been on guard all alone at the cliff top, came silently down the trail, his face as impassive as ever.

"Isn't time to leave yet, Bennie," said Mack Dunbar as

he wiped the sweat from his face.

"That's what you think, Skipper," said Bennie. "The rest of them Japs are up there in the fog, calling out to each other, stumbling around looking for their missing buddies, I guess."

"Let them come," said Mike Pucci. He slapped the breech of the twenty millimeter.

"No," said Mack. "The racket this gun would make would carry out to sea and warn that sub. We can't risk it." He looked up toward the unseen cliff top high above them in the concealing fog. "There are only about thirty of them left. Hardly enough to bother with. If we can get back to Adak in time, we can warn the landing force to expect a few Japs here. On the other hand, that sub out there can raise hob with our ships."

"And with us," said Smitty.

Mack began to fill his pipe with the thoughtful expression that usually accompanied it.

"Look out for trouble," whispered Gary to Bob.

Mack lighted his pipe and looked at his tiny crew. "Those Japs have been trying to signal that sub for days. That's my guess. That sub has been expecting signals. Maybe it wants to come in and take off those boys, or perhaps land more of them."

Gary swallowed hard and raised his eyes upward.

Mack blew out a smoke ring. "Let's get this gun aboard and mounted. We just might need it one of these days."

It was a severe strain on the tired men to get the disassembled gun into the powerboat and take it out to the side of *Otter*, where it had to be swung aboard by the boom, but the power winch could not be used because of the noise. Therefore, she was swung aboard by a block and tackle powered with muscle instead of by mechanical

172

means. Mike Pucci and Smitty instantly set to work to bolt it to the deck and assemble it.

By the time *Otter* was ready for sea, the tide had filled the cove. Bob Dunbar coiled a line and hooked it around a belaying pin, then turned to say something to Gary, who was tightening a stay. The words died in his mouth. He could plainly see the lip of the cliff high above them. An hour before that time it had been fully concealed by the mist. The wind was whispering from the sea, driving the fog inland. There were still some hours of daylight left, enough for the Japanese sub to see them if they emerged from the cove.

" It can't be helped, boys," said Mack Dunbar. " Keep your weapons handy, lads." He looked fore and aft, and up to the tips of the masts, before he climbed into the pilot-house. There was little time to be lost. Once that powerful diesel started turning over, the barking exhaust echoing from the close-in cliffs that surrounded the cove would alert anyone within a mile or so of the cove. Each man knew his station. Mack Dunbar was in command, with Thor Andreason at the wheel. Jim Brannon was in sole charge of the engine. Mike Pucci and Smitty manned the forward twenty millimeter gun. Jesse Easter manned the after fifty caliber machine gun, aided by Baldy. Chuck MacIver stood on the starboard wing of the bridge, while Bennie Dutton held the port wing. Gary Lunt was up forward, with his lead line coiled and ready. Bob Dunbar was in the crow's nest, feeling like a target in a turkey shoot.

There was a breathless hesitancy in the cold and foggy air. It seemed to grow very quiet — quieter than it had ever been in that isolated cove. Each man was at his post. The fog was clearing away from the cliff. The ringing of

173

the engine-room telegraph broke the brooding quiet. A moment later the big diesel coughed, spluttered, then roared unsteadily into full life. The sound of the exhaust slammed thunderously back and forth within the walls of the cove.

There was little time to allow the engine to warm up thoroughly. Mack Dunbar waved a hand to Gary Lunt, who instantly started the power winch on the forward deck to draw the anchors from the sandy beach and drag them, dripping, from the shallow water to hang at the hawseholes. *Otter* did not move. Her forefoot still lightly held the bottom. The engine-room telegraph rang again. Slowly, almost imperceptibly, the vessel went astern until the transom was almost touching the sheer rock face of the cove wall. The propeller churned as *Otter* started forward and swung about slowly to head for the cove mouth, her blunt bows clearing the other cove wall by a matter of several feet.

There was no help for it now. *Otter* was committed to the open sea once she cleared the cove. Fair weather or foul, Japanese submarine or no, she was heading home.

14

THE huge headland to port seemed to lean over *Otter* as she moved at a snail's pace through the fifty-foot channel that led tortuously to the open sea, the barking of her exhaust almost deafening as it echoed back and forth between the cliffs. There were other sounds, muffled beneath the exhaust and the washing of the cold seas against the battered hull of the vessel. The cocking of guns, twenty millimeter, fifty caliber, rifles and pistols, could not be heard except by those who cocked them.

The open sea breathed a vast mouthful of chilling fog into the channel, filling it from side to side, flowing about *Otter* until the stem could not be seen from the stern. There was nothing to do but let *Otter* have her head, as a horseman lets his horse have its head when they are lost in a storm. She seemed to hesitate, then footed steadily through the channel, keeping both walls as far away as possible.

Miraculously the vessel was free of those almost unseen cliffs, meeting the heavy wash of the seas. She plunged and wallowed a little, as though unsteady on her feet after being ashore so long. Soon she seemed to surge forward to meet the open seas she loved so well.

Bob Dunbar looked down and saw a needle-edged rock, capped with swirling white foam, pass by not a fathom from *Otter's* side. One thrust by that menace and *Otter* would never recover. He raised his head and could see quite a distance out to sea, although the rest of the vessel and her lower masts were shrouded in the fog. His eyes widened and his throat dried. There offshore, not more than half a mile away, rolling heavily in the ground swell, was the big I-Boat. On her forward deck he could see a small airplane, float equipped, poised on a catapult. There were other unpleasant things to see. A heavy gun abaft the conning tower and a cluster of automatic weapons showed behind the periscopes. Men moved about the sea-washed decks. If the fog and the cold of Amchitka had bitten to Bob's bones with chilling penetration, it was nothing like the iciness that struck him now.

He looked down at the dim bridge. " Skipper! " he yelled. " I-Boat! Half a mile! Dead ahead! "

Mack Dunbar cupped his hands about his mouth. " How far does the fog extend offshore? "

" She lies just beyond the fogbank. I don't think we can be seen." He smiled wanly. " Unless they can see just little ol' me up here, Skipper."

Otter slowed to dead ahead, barely keeping way against the surf and offshore wind. In a matter of half an hour or more the wind would roll up the fog like a window curtain and blow it across the big island astern of *Otter*, leaving the small vessel helplessly exposed in the clear air.

" They're ready to launch a floatplane," called Bob.

" That's all we need," said Chuck MacIver.

Mack Dunbar rubbed his weather-beaten jaws. He had to make a decision and make it quickly, or lose ship and crew.

Something caught Bob's eye from the right. He turned. A white flare was soaring up through the fog to burst with

176

a faint plopping sound just above the upper layer of the drifting mist. A moment later a red flare burst lower than the first flare. A third flare soared up, this time a white one. He turned and stared out at the submarine. He jerked out his binoculars and focused them on the big submersible. The chill crept through his body again as the close view of the sub seemed to swim into the powerful lenses of the glasses. The men were still working about the plane. Evidently none of them had seen the flares, and Bob realized that the sub was too low in the water for anyone to see the flares through the fog. If they got that plane into the air, the pilot would be able to see flare signals with little trouble.

Bob leaned over the edge of the crow's nest. "Flares from near the cove where the abandoned sub lies, sir. Three of them. White, red, and white in that order, about one minute intervals. I can plainly see the sub. They don't seem able to see the flares, sir. But if they launch that plane, the pilot can hardly miss them. He'll be launched any minute now, Skipper."

There was a deathly silence on *Otter* except for the sound of the engine. Every man on deck looked up at Bob, then back at Mack Dunbar. Mack looked over the side. Here and there through the rifting pea soup he could see fanged rocks thrusting themselves up above the seas. He reached inside the pilothouse and drew out the awkward-looking Japanese flare pistol. He snapped open the breech and inserted a flare. For a long moment he looked from one man to another and about his beloved little craft. Then he raised the pistol and fired it out toward the open sea. The flare shot up and burst in the clear air at the upper edge of the fogbank. Bob turned his glasses toward the sub once again. He could see the white of the

177

faces turned toward the place where the flare had exploded. A moment later the red flare burst almost in the same place. Time enough to reload the smoking pistol and fire the last of the flares — a white one this time. The die was cast.

The submarine turned awkwardly and slowly in the surging seas and began to wallow her way toward the unseen shore. Bob wondered if they could see him standing in that exposed crow's nest, half concealed by the fog that was thinning all the time before the cold breath of the wind.

The I-Boat was heading almost directly for *Otter*, hidden in the friendly mist. The seas foamed back from her sharklike bows. Bob crouched lower in the crow's nest, although he knew it was a foolish thing to do. There was no protection at all behind the thick-painted canvas of the crow's nest.

" How does she head, Bob? " called out Mack Dunbar.

" Right at us, sir! " called Bob.

Otter was in an area encircled at fifty to one hundred yards by slimy black rocks over which the seas constantly broke. Her engine was just turning over enough to keep her from drifting. The Japanese on the I-Boat could not hear *Otter*'s diesel above the barking of their own diesel exhaust and the noise of the breaking waves.

A puff of smoke came from the deck of the sub, and the little floatplane shot low over the water, heading out to sea away from the fog, like a wasp bent on mischief.

" Plane launched! " called down Bob. " Heading out to sea! "

The submarine was barely moving now as she neared the fogbank. Men stood at her bows, one of them with a lead line in his hands.

"Where away?" called Mack.

"Dead ahead, sir. At the edge of the fogbank."

Mack raised the pistol and fired another white flare. It burst directly over the I-Boat. A red flare and another white flare soared up. The sub moved a little faster. Already the fog was wreathing about it, covering the low decks, but the conning tower and periscopes still thrust themselves about it. Bob could see the white faces of men on her bridge staring over the wind screen toward the unseen shore. Mist wreathed and swirled between the submarine and *Otter*. Then, as though a conjure man had created the vision of the approaching sub, only to make it disappear by sleight of hand, or magical incantation, the I-Boat was gone.

The plane was droning its slow way toward fogbound East Cape. The wind was driving the reluctant fog closer and closer to the coast.

There was no need to give commands on the deck of *Otter*. Mike Pucci thrust his shoulders into the semicircular rests of the twenty millimeter gun and swung it to face toward the oncoming submarine. Smitty stood by with a spare drum of cartridges. On the afterdeck of the superstructure Jesse Easter set his back into the hooped rest and swung the heavy water-cooled fifty caliber machine gun to aim toward the general direction of the approaching submarine. Chuck MacIver had a submachine gun poised in his big brown hands.

Bob peered down into the fog. Unless the sub had stopped, or gone astern, she should be within a hundred yards or so of *Otter*, which was waiting there in the heaving seas like an unarmored retiarius gladiator armed only with net and trident spear facing a secutor wearing breastplate, heavy helmet, and leg and arm armor, carrying

179

sword and shield. Speed and agility against weight and strength.

Bob suddenly saw something looming darkly in the fog off the starboard bow, so close there was no mistaking what it was. It was the sharp bow of the submarine moving ever closer to *Otter*. She was just making steerageway as she felt her course through the blinding fog. A seaman stood at the very tip of the bow, casting the lead even as Gary Lunt had done when Bob had taken the powerboat close inshore seeking an anchorage for *Otter*.

There was no need to warn Mack Dunbar. He waved a hand at Mike Pucci. The twenty millimeter stuttered into life, lashing the water with its slugs. They tattooed a pattern of holes from the submarine's bow aft toward the conning tower, felling the leadsman on the way. The slugs swept the bridge of the submarine, shattering the wind screen, striking faces, slamming into the periscope standards behind the bridge. Back and forth Mike sprayed his deadly metallic broom, driving seamen over the side, some alive and some dead, to die anyway in the icy, killing waters.

Japanese seamen scuttled for the trio of twenty-five millimeter guns mounted abaft the periscopes. At that instant Jesse Easter opened up with his roaring fifty caliber machine gun, sweeping it back and forth in a small arc, pouring slugs into the seamen and their guns.

The submarine still had way on it. She drove on toward *Otter*, impelled not only by her propeller but also by the scend of the sea. Men rolled about on the wet decks and slid helplessly into the sea. A twenty-five millimeter gun stuttered into life. Slugs churned the water between the *Otter* and the submarine, and then suddenly they stitched a way up the ironbark sheathing of the vessel to sweep

180

across the well deck, parting shrouds and stays. Jesse Easter caught that gun in a pattern of bullets, and as the Japanese fell back dead from the gun the weight of his body tilted it upward, still firing. Slugs smashed into the thick mast, and Bob heard some of them rip through the canvas sheathing of the crow's nest. Something plucked eagerly at his parka and then the stream of slugs shot upward and died away.

Otter was under way now at half speed, moving toward the oncoming submarine, guns rattling and smoking from every part of the vessel. There was no chance for the Japanese to get the afterdeck gun in action. They tried only once, and Mike Pucci cleaned them from the bullet-riddled superstructure deck. Now the sub swung to port and came directly at *Otter* again. She seemed to have no one at her helm; no one *alive*, that is. Her shark bow seemed to eat up the distance, and then it struck *Otter* a glancing blow that heeled her over, so that water washed over the port rail. Smitty was hurled down into the well deck, where he lay still. Gary staggered back against the winch and fell over it, but Mike Pucci, the second-rater, as Mack Dunbar had called him, stayed at his gun until the big ammunition drum ran dry, pouring a hail of slugs into the conning tower, now so close. Chuck MacIver leaned over the bridge as a knot of screaming men jumped for the side of the *Otter* in a wild attempt to board her. His submachine gun chattered and spat smoke, and the boarding attempt was broken up. The sub swept past *Otter* and it seemed as though her speed was increasing, as though she wanted to get away from her persistent tormentor.

Bob could see down onto the sub's bridge. A man was trying to get to one of the twenty-five millimeter guns.

Bob raised his rifle, sighted quickly, squeezed off, and felt the hard and merciless kick of the rifle against his shoulder. The Japanese fell out of sight, blocking the open hatchway that led below to the conning tower interior.

Otter headed for sea with a wreath of powder smoke rising from her decks as she kept up the hail of fire. Mack Dunbar climbed into the mizzen shrouds like Farragut at Mobile Bay to look back at the submarine. The submarine was slowing down, water boiling up from beneath her stern as she attempted to reverse herself away from the still unseen shore. Slowly she made stern way, and men poured out on her decks as *Otter* began to draw out of range and the area between the two vessels was clouded with smoke and thick with fog.

"Come about!" yelled Mack to Thor Andreason.

Bob caught a glimpse through a pilothouse window of the white, set face of Thor, who had failed twice under fire while a crew member of *Otter*. He was staring dead ahead.

"Come about!" roared Mack Dunbar.

Thor seemed to shake as though in the grip of an ague. Then his hands tightened on the wheel and he slowly turned the *Otter* to head back into the blinding fog and smoke.

"Come down from there!" yelled Mack to Bob.

Bob wasted no time. He came down the ratlines and hardly felt them beneath his feet. He ran to the twenty millimeter gun just as Mike finished placing a fresh drum of ammunition on it. Smitty lay facedown on the deck and did not move. Gary had limped painfully to the starboard scuppers and sat there gripping his leg, a dazed look on his face.

"You'll ram her!" yelled Bennie Dutton to Mack Dunbar.

"That's the idea!" said Mack. "*Otter* has acted as an ice breaker. She can do it again."

"Against steel?"

Mack grinned. "You have any better ideas?"

Bennie shrugged. He leaned over the rail, rifle ready, watching for the first sight of the sub.

Bob looked over his shoulder and his heart dropped like a sounding lead. The conning tower was dead ahead of them. Men were grouped about the afterdeck gun, training it toward *Otter* as she forged swiftly toward them, oblivious of the danger. The submarine was slowly swinging away from disaster.

"Open fire!" commanded Mack Dunbar hoarsely.

The twenty millimeter gun stuttered into noisy life. The fifty caliber machine gun had too much defilade to fire as yet. Mike swept the sub, scattering the screaming gun crew, plastering the bridge and conning tower, then back again along the decks.

Closer and closer drew *Otter*, and Bob realized she was almost at her full speed of twelve knots, the engine banging away for all it was worth. Rocks showed to port and starboard. No one but a superlative pilot such as Mack Dunbar, and a cool hand at the helm such as Thor Andreason, could have kept *Otter* from ripping out her wooden bottom on those rocks. She passed between them and got a fair shot at the submarine and her demoralized crew.

"Replacement drum!" shouted Mike.

Bob removed the empty drum and clapped the last drum of ammunition on the hot, smoking gun. When he looked again he saw that *Otter* was so close that he could not see the sub's low-lying hull, only the bullet-pocked conning tower.

"Down!" yelled Mack Dunbar.

183

Every man except helmsman Thor Andreason hit the deck. Twenty-five millimeter slugs poured over the bows of the *Otter* from one of the guns abaft the conning tower as the Japanese made a last-ditch stand. They ripped into the mast, tore the shrouds, pocked the forward face of the superstructure, and stitched a deadly seam up the concrete-protected pilothouse, shattering windows and pouring into the pilothouse. Through it all Thor kept his post, steering as steadily as though on a calm lake during peacetime.

Then *Otter* struck directly opposite the conning tower, riding up the outer hull, biting savagely into the superstructure deck, battering into the rounded side of the salt-streaked conning tower. *Otter* shuddered and slid back into the moiling water while Mike leaped to his gun and opened up at point-blank range. As *Otter* swung away and felt the drive of her screw, she described a wide circle, missing rocks by inches, while machine gunner Jesse Easter and every man on deck who could shoot opened up on the submarine. No man could live on the deck or the bridge of the damaged submarine. Somehow she kept under way, but she could not avoid the *Otter* as the sturdy craft headed relentlessly for her again, striking this time right at her stern, smashing the port diving fin, grinding on to crumple the rudder and smash the whirling propeller, riding clear over the low-lying stern while gunfire filled the opaque air with a hellish din and gun barrels smoked and turned electric blue from the intense heat of their firing.

The sub struck and struck hard, grinding against the fanged rocks, shearing tough steel as though it was wet paper, until the boat came to a halt and began to tilt to port, slowly at first, then faster as the hungry, icy seas poured into the pressure hull, driving the remaining members of the crew out onto the sloping deck like ants from a disturbed heap. One by one they leaped into the killing water.

" Cease fire! " roared Mack Dunbar. " Stand by to pick up survivors! "

There weren't many of them. Some had stood on the riddled and shattered deck as the I-Boat made her last crash dive and went down with her to her final resting place. Others deliberately turned their backs on *Otter* and swam toward the dimly seen shore. They wouldn't last long. Twelve minutes was the average time to live in those waters. One of them swam alongside *Otter* and his officer's cap was plain to see. As Bob threw him a line he raised a hand out of the water, aiming an automatic pistol at Bob. An instant before he fired, Bennie Dutton raised a submachine gun and half emptied a drum into the officer who went down in a swirl of oil-stained and bloody water.

Then *Otter* moved slowly astern, with four bedraggled, oil-blackened Japanese seamen lying on her well deck, coughing their insides out, while Chuck and Bennie stood guard over them with cocked submachine guns. A vast swirl of debris broke the oily surface of the waters — cork from the insulation of the submarine, life jackets, bits of wood, uniforms, and a limp body here and there.

The site of the wreck faded away in the fog. *Otter* came about and headed offshore, down by the bows, taking water fast. Her pumps thudded into life. A big canvas stopper was prepared and lowered over her bows to try to stop some of the water from pouring through the split seams and shattered planking. The wind had strengthened and was now driving the fog back to the looming cliffs west of East Cape, but the sea was not making up yet in any strength.

Bob finished bandaging Gary's knee and looked up. Above the sound of the engine and the washing of the seas had come yet another sound. A faint droning. He looked up to see flying toward them the little floatplane that the I-Boat had launched. He had completely forgotten about it. The plane banked as though to get a better look at them and droned on toward where the submarine had launched the plane.

"Why didn't he attack?" said Gary as he pulled himself to his feet.

Mike Pucci looked up at the retreating plane. "They carry no armament," he said quietly. "Just the pilot and a radio."

"Look at him!" said Bennie. "He's circling over the area where we sank the sub."

Mack Dunbar took his pipe from his mouth. "He'll see the debris," he said. "Maybe he'll even see the hull below the water. He's high enough."

The plane banked and flew low over the scene of the fight. Back and forth he flew as *Otter* slogged on toward East Cape. The plane suddenly began to climb. Which way would he go now that his submarine had been destroyed? Kiska was not too far away and he'd have enough gas to make it. Slowly he banked and headed back toward *Otter*.

"And me without a round to fire," said Mike disgustedly.

"Where's Jesse?" demanded Mack Dunbar from the bridge.

"Sick as a dog," said Baldy from the afterdeck. "Jesse can lick anything except seasickness."

"Let me handle that gun, Baldy," said Mike.

186

Baldy turned slowly. "Are you kidding? I remember Dutch Harbor last June when some of those boys plastered us and we didn't even have a BB gun to shoot back at 'em. I remember Nels Andreason standing right where I'm standing now and being blown to bits. No, sir! Ol' Baldy is going to handle this gun and I'd like to see anyone stop me. All you boys are heroes and a cook gets nothing but complaints. This time I'm going to get me a Jap!"

There was no use trying to maneuver *Otter* out of the way. She was too slow, with water heavy in her battered hull. Yet the Jap had no way of attacking the vessel. *No way except with the plane itself.*

The plane banked, tilted, and shot down toward the *Otter*. Baldy settled himself within the hooped backrest, shifting his feet forward on each side of the pedestal mount until his back was about a foot from the deck, while he sighted on the downcoming plane. Every eye was on that little plane as it gathered speed in its dive. At the last instant, when it seemed as though Baldy had gone to sleep, he slapped his palm down on the butterfly trigger and the blunt nose of the big machine gun spat flame and smoke. Tracers leaped in an arc across the darkening sky to meet the nose of the plane. For a moment it kept on its course, then it shuddered convulsively. Bits of material flew from the motor and the wings. It raised a little, and Baldy sowed a seam of slugs from nose to tail. It fell off on one wing, and the machine gun slammed slugs into the wings. One of the wings broke off, and the plane went into a wild, erratic spin toward the heaving surface of the sea. Baldy stopped firing as the plane plunged into the water.

They watched the wreckage. A head appeared from the water and the pilot swam toward the shattered debris to crawl out upon it. He perched there, soaked to the skin, shivering in the rising wind as *Otter* turned slowly toward him. As they drew closer they could see the white scarf bound about his head, marked with Japanese writing. He stared fixedly at them, then drew out a pistol. He fired three times and the slugs sang thinly across the deck of *Otter*.

Mack Dunbar nodded to Thor at the wheel. Thor turned the vessel away from the sinking wreckage. The gap widened and the darkness began to come down upon the cold, heaving seas. Far astern was the downed plane with the pilot hanging on to it as it sank lower and lower. In a little while there was nothing to see astern but the wide wake of the vessel and the whitecaps of the waves.

At dawn, *Otter* wallowed past the tip of East Cape, scraps of patched and weathered canvas spread to steady her, soaked canvas patch slapped against her broken bows, bullet-torn rigging flying like Irish pennants in the wind.

Off to the east appeared a modern destroyer, slamming through the rough seas toward *Otter*, her signal lamp blinking rapidly. Far beyond her were many other ships, vaguely seen in the grayness of sky and water.

Smitty, his head wreathed in a bandage, flicked the shutter of the signaling lamp as the destroyer stopped signaling. The response came quickly. Smitty grinned as he turned to Mack Dunbar. "We're supposed to get this *tub* out of these waters. We've been listed as lost at sea."

"Anything else?" said Mack quietly as he filled his pipe.

Smitty hesitated. "Well," he said uncertainly.

"Go on!"

"He says there's a shooting war going on here, no place for a fish trap like ours to be playing Navy."

Mack Dunbar nodded. He looked down at his tired, dirty-faced crew. "Smitty, you signal back to that tin can

188

that if they'll be *kind* enough to send a whaler over to us, with some *armed* men aboard it, we'll be *very* happy to transfer to their keeping four sailors of his Nipponese Majesty's Imperial Japanese Navy, from an I-Class submarine sunk by this *fish trap* while that tin can was playing like *it* was Navy."

Later that cold dawn, as *Otter* slugged her way east, homeward bound at last, down by the head and with a ten-degree list to starboard, she passed, at a respectful distance, four large gray transports, escorted by lean destroyers and a cruiser, heading in toward Constantine Harbor. It was Task Force Amulet laden with men of the Alaskan Defense Command ready to occupy Amchitka Island preparatory to building a new air base only sixty miles east of enemy-occupied Kiska. Alaskan Scouts and tough infantrymen had landed earlier to deal with the handful of demoralized Japanese left behind by *Otter*. It was January 12, 1943, a little more than seven months after the Japanese bombing attacks on Dutch Harbor. The end of the Japanese occupation of the westernmost Aleutians would soon be in sight.

A signaling lamp blinked on the bridge of the cruiser. It was the flagship of the escorting vessels. "Cannot afford an escort for you," it blinked. "Well done, *Otter*!"

Mack Dunbar lighted his pipe. "Since when does *Otter* need an escort," he growled.

Otter dipped deeply, rolled with the hard punch of the next wave, and rose to the crest, a little slowly it is true, but she did rise. She was on her way home, and the safety of her motley crew depended on her, as it always had. She'd get them there, as she always had.

The gray-painted YP boat swung at her anchor in Dutch Harbor as the brand-new destroyer came slowly into the harbor at dusk to anchor within hailing distance of the YP. On the port wing of the patrol boat's little bridge stood a square-hewn chief petty officer, a pipe clamped in his jaw, watching the tin can as she was moored. It was the bitter spring of 1945.

"Hey, Chief!" called out a fresh-faced sailor on the fantail of the destroyer. "Aren't you afraid to take that fish trap outa this harbor? Gets mighty rough out there, Chief. Might even be a Jap or two out there on a rubber boat! Hawww!" The kid was hardly more than nineteen and he reminded the chief of someone he had known aboard the patrol craft not so long ago, before she had been purchased by the Government and converted into a patrol boat. Kid by the name of Gary Lunt.

A row of grinning swabbies were listening to the kid. With such an audience he could hardly stop. "Hey, Chief!" he called out again. "That thing sitting on the bottom? Looks like it can hardly float!"

The chief turned slowly and reached inside the pilothouse. A long flashlight was in his hand. He flicked it on and turned the beam toward the stumpy funnel of the patrol boat. Plainly seen in the yellowish circle of light were two painted Japanese flags and next to them were silhouettes, one of a float plane and the other of a big Jap I-Class submarine. The light was held on the two flags and their silhouettes just long enough for every swabbie and officer on the tin can to see them, then it flicked out. Mack Dunbar emptied his pipe over the side of the YP, once named *Otter,* and went below.

Mack sat down in the messroom and poured a cup of coffee. He took out a wad of worn letters and spread them before him. There was no need to read them. He knew the contents of every one of them by heart. One letter was from his nephew Bob Dunbar, now a signalman second class on a destroyer somewhere in the Central Pacific, with news of Gary Lunt, who was a gunner's mate on the same ship. Another letter was from Gunner's Mate First Class Michael Pucci, now serving aboard an aircraft carrier with his inseparable buddy Homer Smith. A badly written epistle was from Corporal Jesse L. Easter, somewhere in Italy. Jim Brannon had written from Seattle, where he and Baldy Barker were working on a big harbor tug. Chuck MacIver, now Sergeant MacIver, had written from Fort Richardson on the Alaskan Mainland where he and Bennie Dutton were helping to train Army personnel in arctic warfare. The last letter was from Thor Andreason, who was working for the Government in various hospitals demonstrating the skilled use of his artificial hand to other maimed servicemen. It was the one Mack read most often.

A young swabbie poked his head into the messroom. " Chief," he said, " I just received a message that a barge is adrift off Avatanak Island. We're supposed to go look for it. Shall I send back an answer that we're on the way? "

Mack Dunbar stowed the letters back inside his coat and got up. He slewed his hat to a seagoing angle, relighted his pipe, and walked toward the door. " That's what we're here for, kid," he growled. " Tell 'em *Otter* is on the way! "

" *Otter*, Skipper? "

" That's what I said," roared Mack Dunbar. " They know who we are, and if they don't, it's high time they found out! Jump and make it so! "

Otter bobbed easily, tugging at her moorings now and then to test them, eager to get to sea. *To the cold seas beyond . . .*

Bibliography

History of United States Naval Operations in World War II, Samuel Eliot Morison. Volume IV, *Coral Sea, Midway and Submarine Actions May 1942–August 1942.* Volume VII, *Aleutians, Gilberts and Marshalls June 1942–April 1944.* Little, Brown and Company, 1961.

United States Naval Operations in World War II, Theodore Roscoe. United States Naval Institute, December 1949.

Sunk! Mochitsura Hasimoto. Henry Holt & Company, Inc., 1954.

National Geographic, September 1942; August 1943.

Life. Various issues, 1943.

Air Progress Magazine.

Yank Magazine.